THE Art of Running Away

THE Art of Running Away

Sabrina Kleckner

JOLLY
FiSH
PRESS

Mendota Heights, Minnesota

First Edition
First Printing, 2021

Book design by Jake Slavik
Cover design by Ana Bidault (Beehive Illustration)
Cover illustration by Ana Bidault (Beehive Illustration)

Jolly Fish Press, an imprint of North Star Editions, Inc.

This is a work of fiction. Names, characters, places, and incidents are either the product of the author's imagination or are used fictitiously, and any resemblance to actual persons living or dead, business establishments, events, or locales is entirely coincidental.

Library of Congress Cataloging-in-Publication Data (pending)
978-1-63163-577-9

Jolly Fish Press
North Star Editions, Inc.
2297 Waters Drive
Mendota Heights, MN 55120
www.jollyfishpress.com

Printed in Canada

For Paige Pendergrast

This Cat Is More Iconic Than Me

At Glenna's Portraits, we paint people, not cats. But here I am on the first day of summer vacation, sketching a fat orange feline onto canvas paper. I can only guess Dad took on this portrait because the Matthews are regular customers of Glenna's. We don't usually have regulars, because how many paintings of your own face do you really need in your house? But although Melinda and Marilyn Matthews only moved to Crescent Valley three years ago, they've commissioned over ten portraits from us. Their kids, their grandkids, Melinda's mother, Marilyn's uncle . . . the list goes on. So when we got the call last week that they wanted to commission a portrait of the family cat, I wasn't exactly surprised. But also . . . help? The last time I painted a bear, Alicia thought it was a turtle.

Not that it really matters. My job for the shop is to sketch initial ideas on scrap paper—Dad is the only person allowed to handle the expensive canvases used for our final portraits. He did say he might start letting me take on more responsibilities, though, so if I impress him with this cat commission, maybe— maaaaaybe—by the end of the summer, he'll let me do more than ogle the oil paints from the other end of the workshop.

"Maisie, I have an idea for your sketch. The cat should be in space," Alicia says from somewhere behind me. I don't need to glance at her to know she's belly-down on the straw floor of my family's workshop, head buried in The Book, orange curls falling onto the pages.

I consider my composition. I sketched the cat onto the middle of the page, mimicking the pose of the reference photo exactly. I never met Mr. Fluffer in person, but it's clear from the pictures Dad snapped of him that he's a sassy cat. His head is cocked at a "don't you dare photograph my bad side" angle, and every hair on his fluffy body is perfectly groomed.

"Mr. Fluffer wouldn't like space," I counter. "He'd have to wear a space suit, which would cover his fur. He'd definitely be offended if I cover his fur."

"Then how about an abstract background?" Alicia tilts her head, considering. "That way, Mr. Fluffer will be the center of attention. He won't have to compete with anything else."

"Ooh, *yes*. Maybe I'll even suggest black and white to Dad so Mr. Fluffer is the only pop of color on the page." I look up from my sketch for the first time in two hours. "If only we could agree this easily on The Book."

Alicia props herself on her elbows and flips her mane of hair—which definitely rivals Mr. Fluffer's in its magnificence—over her head. It's only after she does this that I see the page she's working on. There are more words than white space, which means I'll barely have any room to illustrate her poem. Seriously? I thought we talked about this.

I jab a finger toward The Book. "You promised to leave half a page open for me!"

"It's just a first draft." Alicia raises both hands in the air like I'm holding a can of spray paint to her chest. "You'll have enough space to draw once I edit."

My skin bristles. If I were covered in as much hair as Mr. Fluffer, it would be standing up all over my body. "Alicia," I say through clenched teeth, "we've talked about this. Write your first drafts on a separate sheet of paper. They're not ready for The Book yet. They're especially not ready to be written in pen!"

I love Alicia to death, but she does *not* have the same grasp on artistry as I do. We've been working on The Book since third grade, and it's basically a jumbled collection of her poetry and my paintings. Three years on, and you'd think she'd know to write her first drafts on practice paper. But Alicia and editing don't really go together. She thinks art should be raw and imperfect. I think art should be polished and calculated. You can see why we run into issues. We can't even agree on a name for The Book, for Fluffer's sake.

I was hoping things would be different this summer. We have three entire months to work on this messy project of our hearts, so if nothing else, I planned for us to have at least agreed on a theme by the time we start seventh grade. Right now, Alicia's poems range everywhere from "Light-Up Shoes Light Up My Heart" to "My Bones Are Fertilized by Sadness." They're awesome, but do they belong in the same story?

I shoot Alicia a glance while pretending to still be examining her latest poem. She won't admit it out loud, but I know she's not as invested in The Book as I am anymore. From September to March, we spent at least three hours every day crowded over the delicate pages, adding ink and paint and words and feelings. But then . . . Alicia started dating Rowan.

I have nothing against Rowan. I know them pretty well because we've had English together for the past few years, which is about as long as Alicia's liked them. But Alicia likes a lot of people. She couldn't stop talking about Isaac Newman in fourth grade, and in fifth grade she took an extra math class just so she could sit next to Erica Sanchez three times a week. Extra math?! I mean, that's dedication right there. But even though she and Erica went to the fifth-grade dance together, Rowan is the first person Alicia's ever asked *out*. Since then, I've only seen Alicia in spatters.

A two-minute conversation before history class. The five-minute walk home from school. Twenty minutes on the phone before bed so we could complain about the geography final exam. We went from spending more time together than apart to one tiny hour in the Glenna's workshop this week. I guess I should have expected this. We've been working on The Book for years, so maybe Alicia's bored of it. But what if it's not The Book Alicia's bored of? I'm not exactly new and exciting, either.

That thought has been burrowing deeper and deeper into my brain over the past few weeks. I want to know if I'm right, if she really *is* bored of me. But every time I open my mouth, I can't get the question past my teeth.

Alicia frowns, like she can tell there's something serious on my mind. I chew on my lip. Before I can decide whether to say anything, Mom blasts into the workshop, scattering my thoughts like an unstable pile of paper.

Mom never walks. She only bursts or barges or blasts. You'd think this would mean she looks like a tornado—wild and out of control—but her grooming rivals Mr. Fluffer's. Her auburn hair is always in a perfect bun that somehow defies gravity by sitting on top of her head. There's never a crack in her polished nails, and even when she spends the day in the workshop with Dad, she manages to walk out without a spot of paint on her. That's never happened to me. I've only been sketching with a pencil today, but somehow there's purple paint in my hair. I swipe the strand behind my ear, hoping Mom won't notice.

She does. Her brows dimple as she picks the vivid color out of the surrounding blond, but instead of telling me to wash up like usual, she turns her attention on Alicia. "It's time for you to go home."

Alicia nods immediately and shuts The Book. She's intimidated by Mom, and I know on the outside Mom looks intimidating. But Mom isn't scary—she's fierce. Similar words, but people don't need a reason to be scary. To be fierce, you need to care. Mom runs the business side of Glenna's. If she didn't dress to perfection, she wouldn't come across as professional to our clients. If she weren't blunt and to the point, she wouldn't get things done as efficiently. I don't always get along with Mom, but I do understand her.

"See you tomorrow," Alicia mutters as she leaves via the big wooden door of the Glenna's workshop. Dad converted the barn into a studio before I was born, but there are still remnants of its previous life left over—the massive door, the slight smell of manure, the metal machine in the corner that I think was once used to milk cows. Otherwise, though, the workshop is pretty modern.

It's painted white and has huge windows across one wall to let in natural light, as well as lamps all across the space that simulate daytime for when we have to work at night. Closest to the door is the sketching station, which is where I work. There are several easels with large sketchbook paper, high-quality graphite pencils, and a file of reference photos that I flip through when I need a new project to work on. Then there's the painting station, where Dad basically lives. He uses oil paint for the portraits, so we also have a drying station. In the far corner, we have what I call the waiting station, which is where finished portraits get fitted with fancy frames and chill by themselves until they're picked up or shipped off to their customers. I love our workshop. I would sleep here if Mom didn't look horrified every time I mentioned it—and if the oil paints didn't smell so strong.

As soon as Alicia is out of earshot, Mom jerks her head in the direction of the main house, which I can barely see through the long grass and descending darkness. "Family meeting," she says, already walking away from me. "Dad's waiting in the living room."

My breath flies away on a gasp. That sounds dramatic, but when it comes to fears, I don't have many. Heights? No problem! Doctor's appointments? Who cares! There are less than a handful of phrases in the entire world that fill me with dread. "Clowns with chain saws" is one. "Family meeting" is another.

Never Sit on the Sapphire Couch

I sit on the sapphire blue couch in the living room, my knee bouncing up and down in time with my heart. Mom and Dad are both silent. For way too long. Whatever this is about, it's going to be horrible.

I let my eyes wander as I wait for someone to talk. The living room hangs with memories—literally. The walls are covered with art: mainly mine and Dad's, but also a few pieces by Mom. Above the couch is a large painting of a sunset, except instead of soft oranges and yellows and pinks, it's made of jagged lines of green and gray and black. The living room is covered in traditional-style landscapes and portraits, so this abstract piece looks a little strange in comparison. I didn't paint it, and it's not Mom's or Dad's style. It took me a few years to realize it must have been done by Calum. Now every time I sit below it, I'm reminded of our first family meeting. Nothing has ever topped it in terms of awfulness, but my parents don't just sit me down on the sapphire couch when they have something *good* to say.

Dad glances at Mom. He has a small paintbrush tucked behind one ear, which looks cool but can't actually be comfortable. His jeans are covered in paint stains old and new, and he looks a little out of place next to Mom's wrinkleless clothes and flawless makeup. If I were a stranger passing them on the street, I'd never guess they were married.

"Maisie, I love that you're so passionate about Glenna's," Mom begins, "It's great that you're working on a book with Alicia, but you're going to be a teenager soon. It's got me thinking that you should spend some time away from art."

I make a noise. It sounds a bit like "huh?" because of all the things I was imagining Mom would say—*You need more friends than just Alicia, Please actually do your summer reading this year, Calum's coming home*—this was not one of them. It takes all my strength not to shoot to my feet. I open my mouth again, and this time I'm more successful in the words department. "You want me to spend time away from art? What does that even mean? We literally run an art shop!"

Mom's eyes move up the wall to where one of my paintings hangs next to Calum's sunset. It's a landscape of the Crescent Valley woods behind our house. I spent a week trying to get the lighting right.

"Piseag, you're so talented. But before you're stuck in a job for the rest of your life, you should try new things. Have some adventures. Figure out what else you like."

I wince at the old nickname. Apparently when I was little, I saw a kitten bathing its wrist with its tongue and I mimicked it for a week or two. Even though it was a million years ago, Mom has called me piseag—Gaelic for "kitten"—ever since. But I'm not a child anymore. I don't need a nickname, and I definitely don't need Mom to decide how I spend my summer.

Mom turns to Dad, like she's waiting for him to back her up. He is determinedly staring at the floor with his lips sealed shut. At least he's not taking Mom's side, but urgh. I could use some help here!

Mom sighs. "This isn't an attack, Maisie, but it's also not a discussion. You need a more well-rounded life. What if, in twenty years, you realize you don't like art as much as you did when you were twelve? What will you do with yourself then, if you have no other skills? You're spending the summer working at your Aunt Lisa's ice cream shop in Edinburgh. I already bought your plane ticket. You leave tomorrow."

I didn't think people's jaws actually dropped in real life, but at the end of that sentence, mine falls to my feet. Okay, not really. But my mouth opens very wide. *"What?"* I jump up from the couch. "You . . . you can't just . . . I've never even met Aunt Lisa! I . . ." I always thought Mom and I were on the same page. She's as invested in Glenna's as I am, so where is this coming from? Just because I'm twelve doesn't mean I'm too young to know who I am. I don't need to spend my summer in another country, scooping ice cream, when I've already found my one true passion. "I need to stay here. Alicia and I—"

"Isn't Alicia dating Rowan from your English class?" Mom asks.

"What does that have to do with anything?"

"Well, I've noticed you spending more time on your own lately. Going abroad will give you something to do besides sulking around the workshop. I don't want you to be lonely—"

"I'm *not*." I cross my arms over my chest. "And even if I was, that doesn't mean I need to go to Scotland! My life is here. I—"

"Còrdaidh Dùn Èideann riut glan." Mom says it like it's the end of the discussion, clapping her palms against her lap for emphasis.

That's the last straw. Mom has been trying to teach me Gaelic since I was a baby, but that doesn't make me Scottish. My home is *here*. In Upstate New York. At Glenna's. Not in some random country across the ocean with an aunt I've never met. "I'm not going," I snap, storming into the hallway.

"Maisie—" Mom's heels clack behind me on the polished floor. "Maisie! Get back here. You can't run away from me—"

She's wrong. As much as Mom wants to finish this conversation, there is one place in our house she never goes. I know she won't follow me when I round the corner, bolt up the stairs, and dash into Calum's room.

Lying Is Bad . . . Or Is It?

I haven't been in Calum's room in over a year, but it looks the same as it always does. White walls, light green rug, wooden bed covered by a gray and black plaid comforter. A few graphic novels are piled on a shelf in the corner, but otherwise it's as neutral as a hotel room. When I was younger, I used to sneak in here all the time, looking for evidence that might explain why my brother ran away when I was six. But the most personal thing about this room is the sign on the door that reads in jagged writing *Get Out*.

The door creaks open. I jump slightly from where I'm perched on the bed, but it's just Dad. "How did you find me?" I ask as he sits next to me.

He raises his eyebrows. I manage a small smile. Of course he knew where to find me. Dad knows me better than anyone. Well, except for Alicia. My fingers twitch on the bedsheets. Since he knows me so well, Dad should realize going to Scotland isn't what I need this summer. He should have stood up for me against Mom.

"She's not trying to hurt you," Dad says like he can read my thoughts. Or maybe my confusion is obvious. "This isn't a punishment. You know that, right?"

I shrug, because actually no, I don't. Mom's decision to send me away feels like an attack. It smacked me in the face, and I'm still seeing stars. "Does she . . . think I'm not good enough? To work at Glenna's?"

"Honey, no, that's not it at all." Dad puts an arm around my shoulders. "You're a fantastic artist. Every time we deliver a portrait to a client and they're especially pleased, Mom tells them how you drew the initial sketch. *My twelve-year-old daughter . . .* You should hear the pride in her voice."

I stare hard at his face, looking for signs of a joke. Nothing about that was funny, but I find it very hard to believe. "Mom really says that to people?" I mutter, more to myself than to Dad. Mom is so busy running Glenna's that I don't see her often, and when I do, the only words she has time for are critiques. *Get that paint out of your hair. Sit up straight. The left eye isn't to scale. Why did you sketch the chair like that?* I know she loves me, but Dad thinks she's *proud* of me? Any other day, this news would make me inflate a few inches off of Calum's bed. Today, they twist my insides into a knot. "If she really thinks so much of me, why is she sending me away?"

Dad's fingers stop rubbing my shoulder. "You know how dedicated she is to Glenna's. She loves the shop, but sometimes I think she feels consumed by it." He sighs. "We'd be thrilled for you to take over the business one day. Of course we would. But you should never let Glenna's become all you are."

I frown. I don't feel consumed by art. I *am* art. Maybe that sounds kind of ridiculous, but my brain is always composing, rearranging, melding the world into stories I want to paint. I love that about myself. It's what makes me special. Dad should understand this. After all, he's an artist, too.

"Do you agree with her? That I need to leave Glenna's for a whole summer?"

Dad breaks my gaze. He'd rather spend a few hours painting away his frustrations than face a confrontation head-on. It's infuriating.

"I agree you should have interests outside of art," he says finally. "I love my job, but I also love going to the arcade with you, and hiking on the weekends, and movie nights with Mom. I told Mom she could enroll you in a camp here or that you could join a sport with Alicia. I don't think you need to spend the summer in Scotland to find other interests. But you know how Mom is— once she has an idea in her head, there's nothing we can do to stop her going through with it."

"You could have tried." Mom won't listen to me. Even if I write a whole essay explaining why it's wrong to send me away, she won't take me seriously. But Dad is her equal. She'll hear him out if he speaks up . . .

Dad's hand drops off my shoulder. "I know you're angry, Maisie, but please don't snap at me."

I throw up my arms. "You never stand up for me, even when you know I'm right! Maybe if you did more than just sit there, Mom wouldn't have bought the plane ticket without talking to me first." My fingers clench until the fabric of my brother's comforter bunches into my palms. "If you didn't just sit there, maybe Calum wouldn't have run away!"

I regret the words as soon as they're out of my mouth. We don't talk about Calum. Well, Mom and Dad sometimes whisper about him when they think I'm not around, but even surrounded by the echo of him in this room, it feels weird to hear his name in the air. I don't think I've said it out loud since that first family meeting six years ago, and I wouldn't have said it now if my hands weren't knotted in his blankets. Dad jerks back like I've slapped him. "Maisie—" His voice is edged with anger, but also with hurt.

A gross feeling bubbles inside me, but it's not directed at Dad. It's directed at *me*. As annoyed as I am at my parents, I crossed a line. I thought saying something awful would make me feel better, but now I'm too scared to look Dad in the eye, to take in the damage I caused.

"Sorry," I whisper to my feet. I jump off the bed and sprint out of Calum's room, slamming the door behind me.

●●●

"You're going *where*?" Alicia exclaims.

After my fight with Dad, I snuck over to Alicia's house. She's my neighbor, but there's so much distance between the houses in Crescent Valley that it's a good ten-minute walk to her place. I still feel icky about what I said, so I skip over the part about Calum as I catch her up on everything that happened after she left the workshop. While I talk, I stare out Alicia's windows. Her room is at the top of a spire. As a result, she has floor-length windows across all four walls and a skylight on her ceiling. It's breathtaking at sunset, and so different from the rest of the houses in our area. Her dad's an architect, and he made a lot of adjustments to the space when they moved in. As I watch the stretches of green countryside turn fiery red, some of the stress in my throat and chest lessens.

When I finish talking, Alicia is quiet. I go to where she's lying on her bed and nudge her shoulder. "You always have something to say. Tell me what to do!"

She blinks up at me. "What is there to do? Your parents already bought the plane ticket. You're leaving *tomorrow*. Nothing will change their minds."

The way she says it . . . I bite my lip.

"What is that?" Alicia asks.

"What?"

She sticks her chin at me. "You've been acting all moody lately. It happened four times last week and twice today—you got quiet in the workshop earlier, and now you're looking at me like I killed your cat. You don't even have a cat, so I'm very freaked out. Did you have a secret one I somehow killed and now you're mad at me? I didn't mean to kill your fake secret cat!"

Even when I'm sad and angry, Alicia is somehow always able to make me laugh. I snort, then try to rein in my smile. "That's the weirdest thing you've ever said, and you've said a lot of things."

She throws a pillow at me. "Why won't you tell me what's wrong?"

I guess now is the best time to do it. Worst-case scenario, Alicia confirms she's bored of me, and I'll be able to escape to Scotland with my hurt feelings for a few months. Best-case scenario, this has all been in my head, and she'll say I've been worrying for nothing. I stare out the window, watching the sun dip below the horizon. In a few minutes, the world will go dark. A few hours after that . . .

I will probably be on a plane.

"If I go to Scotland, you can spend all summer with Rowan. You won't have to see me or work on The Book. Do you want that?" I ask very quietly.

There's silence for a beat. Two. Three. Oh God. If she were going to deny it, she would have done so already. My stomach drops. Alicia is kind of my only friend. I mean, there are people I hang out with at school, but instead of doing homework at their houses or joining after-school clubs, I always just go home to do work for Glenna's. It's never bothered me before, but now that my only friend is abandoning me . . .

I'm still staring hard out the window, so I don't see Alicia reaching for me until she grabs my wrist. I shriek as she pulls me onto the bed with her, wrapping her arms around mine and hugging me like she used to when we were babies. Alicia might not be my real sister, but we always acted more like siblings than I ever did with Calum.

"Maisie! *That's* why you've been acting all weird? Oh my God!" She shakes my shoulder. "How could you think I'd want you to leave? You are of course the best person in the universe, so without you I will be an anguished blob in my bed all summer. Except I won't have time to be an anguished blob, because I think your parents have been talking to mine. At dinner Dad said he signed me up for tennis lessons. Can you imagine *me*? Doing *tennis*? With, like, that big flyswatter thing and everything?"

I shove her arm. "It's called a tennis racquet. Please tell me you know it's called a tennis racquet!"

"Of course I do. I'm trying to make a point!"

I shake my head in fake disappointment. Most people have nightmares about creepy monsters and chain-saw murderers; Alicia's bad dreams involve doing push-ups and running laps. She purposely wears the wrong shoes to gym class every day so she doesn't have to participate. Picturing her sprinting up and down—sweating her eyes out and cursing under her breath—is hilarious. I kind of want to paint it. Maybe I will for her birthday. She'll kill me, but it will be worth the look of horror on her face.

Her eyes grow more serious. "I know I've been spending more time with Rowan lately, but it's not because I don't want to be around you. I just . . . I have no idea what I'm doing. Like, when Rowan doesn't text me back after five minutes, is it because they already want to break up, or because they're eating dinner? If I ask them about it the next day, do I seem desperate? Or is it cute?"

I frown. Alicia always seems so sure of herself when it comes to friends and crushes and general being-a-human things. I didn't realize she was worried about Rowan, but maybe that's my own fault. Now that Alicia's dating, there's this distance between us that's never been there before. I don't know how to close it. I don't know if I can. So instead of asking tons of questions about her relationship, I've kind of been ignoring it.

Alicia hugs me again. "Don't fight it," she says, and I can't tell if she's talking about her monster hug or my exile to Scotland or the depressing thoughts inside my head. Okay, it's not the last one. We're close, but Alicia doesn't have superpowers. "It's just one summer," she prods. "If you can convince your mom it was transformative or whatever, I'm sure she'll leave you alone for the rest of the year. I'll take the next few months to figure out how to date Rowan, and once school starts, we'll be able to work on The Book as much as we used to."

Some of the panic that's been coursing through my body ever since Mom said "Edinburgh" fades away. Alicia's right: It *is* only one summer. Even if I hate Scotland, Mom will probably drop the whole "you need other interests" thing as long as I pretend the next few weeks are a life-changing experience. She dropped the "we're vegetarians" phase after a month, and "we're throwing out the TV" lasted less than five days.

And honestly? Maybe leaving home for a while won't be the worst thing. I don't want to face either of my parents right now—especially not Dad. Just thinking about his face after I mentioned Calum brings bile up my throat. It will be nice to get some space, even if it means leaving the workshop for a few months.

I cover my eyes with my elbow. "Keep me updated on things at home? I want to hear all about tennis."

"Please. I'm throwing that racquet in the fire the first chance I get." Alicia flashes a smile at the ceiling, but it slowly sinks into a frown. "I'm going to miss you."

I hug her one last time. Her thick ginger hair smells familiarly of lavender shampoo and—vaguely—Cheetos. "I'll miss you, too."

Get Me Out of This City

"Look for parrots."

That's the last thing Mom said to me before I boarded the plane for Edinburgh. Not *Goodbye, sweetie!* or *I'll miss you so much!* or *Call every night!*

And okay, I get what she was going for. "Parrots" is more specific than *Look for the middle-aged woman with brown hair* or *Aunt Lisa will be wearing black boots*. But does Aunt Lisa's handbag have a parrot design? Does she wear a parrot necklace? Is she waiting past baggage claim with a *real* parrot?

The answer, I learn as I wheel my suitcase toward the exit doors, is all of the above.

"Maisie!" A tall, broad-shouldered woman envelops me before I can get a good look at her, so my first impression of Aunt Lisa—besides the parrots—is overwhelming floral perfume and enthusiasm that makes my ribs scream. I don't know how she recognizes me: maybe Mom told her I dyed a stripe of my hair pink last week, or she knows the design on my T-shirt is the current featured image on our website.

As soon as the hug ends, the awkwardness begins. "Here!" Before I understand what's happening, Aunt Lisa shoves her pet parrot into my arms.

I'm not expecting it, and when I'm not expecting something, I flail. The parrot smacks the pavement with a sickening *crunch*. I scream, because ohmygod I've been in this country for twenty minutes and I've already killed a thing, and its *eye* popped out, and—

The black orb rolling toward the curb is definitely plastic.

I lower my hand from my mouth as Aunt Lisa picks up the bird. Its feathers are made of floppy fabric; its talons are painted with such sloppy shading that Dad would have banished the artist from our workshop. I have no idea how I thought this parrot was real. Is this what people mean by "jet lag"?

"I'm sorry," Aunt Lisa says. "It was meant to be a gift, but if you don't like stuffed animals—"

"I love it." I force my lips up at the corners and take the bird from her hands. I don't have anything against stuffed animals—my bedroom in Crescent Valley is covered in them. But it's another thing to have to carry one in public when you're going to be a teenager in 104 days.

Yes, I'm counting.

"Shall we get moving?" Aunt Lisa jerks her head at a bus stop on the other side of the road.

I nod. The faster I distance myself from The Parrot Incident, the better.

•••

It takes about thirty minutes to get from the airport to the city. I should be staring out the window, gawking at the new scenery and listening to Aunt Lisa as she rattles off random facts like a tour guide. But my eyes feel like they have weights attached to them, and I can barely lift my neck into a socially acceptable position. Besides, what do you say to the aunt you've never met but will be living with for five weeks?

My top three options:

1. Is your whole house covered in parrots?
2. Will Scottish people care if I drool on the bus?
3. Thanks for inviting me to stay, but why have I never met you before?

I had seven hours of cramped plane time to role-play conversations in my head, but as soon as we lifted into the air, I started to draw. Mom made me promise not to do any work for Glenna's while I'm in Edinburgh, because "you need to find other passions" and blah blah blah. But after she and Dad went to sleep last night, I snuck my best graphite pencils and a small sketchbook into my bag. I'm not about to give up a whole summer of art just for my parents' satisfaction.

Things were awkward this morning when they took me to the airport. Dad didn't bring up our fight in front of Mom—thank God—but it means I left the country with this ugly mess sizzling between us. I fight with Mom enough to know what to say to get her to forgive me, but I can't remember the last time I fought with Dad. Are my words going to hang over me all summer?

I force the thought away as the bus jostles over cobblestones. At least I left things okay with Mom. Though by "okay," I mean she said, "I'll miss you, Piseag!" and I grunted back.

"Maisie?" A hand shakes my shoulder.

I don't realize my eyes are closed until I have to force them back open. As the accents of the other passengers flood my ears,

I'm hit in the face with reality. I'm in Scotland. Glenna's is thousands of miles away. The distance makes my eyes water, and suddenly I feel more lost on this bus than I did soaring over clouds on the plane. I wipe at my eyes with my sleeve as the driver hits the brakes and the doors hiss open. Aunt Lisa helps me lug my suitcase outside, and for a second, my homesickness vanishes. Because this *city*.

It's not like I've never been in a city before. Our town is about three hours from New York City, so Mom, Dad, and I take sightseeing trips every so often. But although New York has its perks, it's noisy and sticky and blaring with artificial light.

Edinburgh is a gingerbread village.

The buildings and streets are gray and cobbled. The statues look old and crumbly, like I could snap off pieces of metal and they would taste like Christmas. The only things missing are snow and gumdrops frosting the roofs. I should have come here in the winter.

Oh, and there's a freaking *castle*. It perches high in the distance, with ancient stone walls zigzagging down the side of a cliff. I didn't think full-blown castles existed anymore, but here one is, just casually chilling in the middle of a city. A bubble of excitement replaces the unease in my chest. I feel like I stepped into a fairy tale. And for some reason—even though I avoided thinking about him in the airport and on the bus and on the plane—this castle makes me think of my brother. From the few whispered conversations I've overheard, I know he lives in London. But has he been to Edinburgh? This castle is worth seeing.

"That's the New Town." Aunt Lisa points behind me to a street that looks more modern. The ground is paved instead of cobbled, and the sidewalk is wide enough for the hordes of people to scuttle from store to store. "I live in the Old Town, close to the university. The walk isn't far, but it's steep."

She's right. By the time we reach our destination, I'm wheezing like I ran up a mountain. My hair sticks to my neck, and my eyes sting with sweat. As pretty as the cobblestones are, the sun bounces off them and into my face, making it difficult to look anywhere but my feet.

Aunt Lisa pulls out her keys. After I've caught my breath, I realize she must live above her ice cream shop. The storefront is loud but unsurprising, considering her parrot fashion choices. The sign reads Unique Sweets in a bold font, and each letter is a different color. Gaudy purple and pink butterflies swirl behind the words, and the bottom half of the window is painted with a meadow scene. The artistry isn't bad, but in my head I'm already coming up with ways to tone down the sign and sharpen the brushwork.

The interior of the shop isn't any subtler. The walls are painted with massive flowers and animals. And the ice cream . . .

"I don't see the point of serving boring flavors," Aunt Lisa says as I examine the menu. "My most popular is Chocolate Sheep. Don't worry," she adds as my eyes widen, "it's not made of actual sheep. I cover the scoops with tiny marshmallows and draw on eyes with black frosting."

"'Reòiteag chaorach seoclaide,'" I say, reading the flavor name. I didn't think many people spoke Gaelic in Edinburgh, so I'm surprised the menu isn't purely in English.

Aunt Lisa's eyes light up. "A bheil Gàidhlig agad?"

"A little."

I don't know why Mom wants me to learn Gaelic. She and Aunt Lisa didn't grow up speaking it—they both got interested in the language when they were around my age and took classes until they were conversational. I might understand Mom's desire to keep the language alive in our house if she ever talked about her childhood, but she rarely mentions Scotland or her sister. It's like as soon as she met Dad at graduate school in New York, she left her roots behind.

Does Aunt Lisa know why Mom doesn't talk about Scotland? Is that a question I can ask on my first day here? Before I can decide whether to go for it, I let out a yawn so huge that it stings the corners of my lips.

Aunt Lisa smiles. "I'll give you the tour tomorrow, but for now let's get you settled." She leads the way up a staircase at the back of the shop and unlocks the door at the top.

As soon as I step inside, the exhaustion in my bones hits me harder than it does when I stay up all night working on a new portrait for Glenna's. Time speeds up: One moment we're passing through the kitchen and over a fluffy carpet. The next, I'm kicking off my shoes in a bedroom and falling onto a soft comforter.

It takes me less than a minute to fall asleep.

Murderers Already?

It's dark when I open my eyes.

Mom told me not to go to bed until at least 9:00 p.m. or my jet lag would go from horrific to unbearable, but there was no way I would have been able to hold out for that long. I don't even remember when my head hit the pillow. I check my phone. It's 11:28 p.m., and I'm wide awake.

Oops.

I sit up, and the noises from the street below consume me: tires scraping stone, muffled singing, strong accents I can't quite understand. I assume the nightlife is what woke me. Crescent Valley is technically a town, but there are more trees than people.

My phone buzzes. When I unlock it, my eyes watering from the sudden brightness, I see I've missed more than one text.

June 19, 9:15 p.m.

Mom: Edinburgh summers can be cold. Did you pack jeans? Your blue jumper is in your wardrobe, but I don't see the pink one. Does that mean it's flung somewhere under your bed? I told you to clean your room before you left.

11:30 p.m.

Me: I brought the pink one.

Mom: And shoes? Did you only pack sandals?
I'm in your room staring at those white
trainers.

Me: It's fine.
Me: I brought my jean jacket and you
know I don't get that cold anyway.

11:33 p.m.

Mom: It's not hip to pretend you're not cold.
You'll be upset if you get sick.

Me: I'm not pretending. Also, no one
says "hip". Good night.

Mom: Good night, Piseag.
Mom: Don't forget to take those
multivitamins I packed you.

I almost send her an eye-roll emoji for using my nickname
when she knows I'm mad at her, but I resist. *Stay on her good side
and she'll leave you alone,* I repeat to myself over and over. Before I
say something I regret, I open my other messages: one from Dad,
three from Alicia.

7:18 p.m.

Dad: Missed you in the workshop today. I
sent your sketch of Mr. Fluffer to Mrs.
and Mrs. Matthews, and they love it!

My fingers freeze. It's such an ordinary text. Does that mean he forgives me for what I said in Calum's room? Or is he ignoring our fight because he doesn't want to face it? I guess I should be relieved if he's ignoring it. But my throat is tight, and I kind of have the urge to respond with *Can't we talk about it?*

Before I can work up the nerve, text bubbles appear on Dad's end.

11:35 p.m.

Dad: I'm not angry about what you said in Calum's room.

Dad: We sprang this Scotland trip on you last minute and emotions were high. But I did want to explain myself better, as I think my intentions got a little lost.

Dad: You'll be in high school soon, and then college, and then at work. It's much harder to try new things when you're weighed down by adult responsibilities.

Dad: What I mean is I agreed with Mom's reasoning for wanting to send you abroad, and so I chose not to intervene. It was a conscious decision, not a default because I didn't care enough to take sides.

Dad: I hope you know I always care when it comes to you.

I breathe out slowly. Dad is careful with his battles. It can be frustrating, because he doesn't just throw his support behind anything (my life would be much easier if he did). But it also means he's always sincere. When he says he's not mad at me, I know he really means it.

> Me: I'm sorry about what I said. There's no way you would have let Calum run away if you could help it.
>
> Me: I'm still thankful you convinced Mom not to make me take that after-school Young Entrepreneur class last year.
>
> Me: And the weekend How To Finance A Small Business seminar. That one especially sounded awful.

Dad: You'll have to learn how to run Glenna's eventually, but those classes did seem a little excessive for a twelve-year-old.

> Me: Mom is a little excessive.

Dad: Maybe, but we love her for it.

> Me: Urgh.
>
> Me: Anyway.
>
> Me: It's late here.

Dad: Go to sleep!
Dad: And have fun in Scotland! I miss you already.

> Me: Miss you, too.

I don't think I've realized how much tension I've been carrying from that fight until it all leaves my body in one big breath. I'm so glad we cleared this up. I hate leaving things unresolved.

After looking over our texts for another moment, I click out of them and open Alicia's.

6:04 p.m.

Alicia: Ummmm.
Alicia: Helloo?!
Alicia: You promised to text as soon as you landed are you dead?!?!

Over the past few months, Alicia hasn't texted as much as she used to. But when she does, her extreme reactions almost make up for the time gap. I'm about to type *Dead in a ditch*, when my fingers are interrupted by a sharp knock.

My heart jumps to my throat. It's nearly midnight, so I doubt whoever is at the front door is a friend of Aunt Lisa's. This is why I can't live in a city. There are so many people stacked on top of each other. Burglars and murderers currently have better access to me than my parents do, and wow, it sucks I'm going to die on my first night away from home . . .

I bolt out of bed—to do what, I'm not sure. Warn Aunt Lisa? Tackle the burglar? Climb out my window and down the side of the building?

(Okay, I know I'm being a little dramatic. But jet lag can do a lot to a brain.)

"Hello?" Aunt Lisa's bright tone colors the dark apartment.

"It's me," a low voice replies. "Where's Maisie? I heard she's staying with you."

My blood leaves my body. I've read this book before. The strange man at the door is probably here to tell me that I'm the long-lost princess of a forgotten country, that I'll be attending a magic school for witches in the fall, or that he's been stalking my Instagram for the past three months and is here to chop me into pieces.

Let's be real—the last option is the most likely. So I do what any (almost) teenager would do. I yank my covers over my head, curl into a ball, and hope I look more like a lumpy pillow than a sweaty girl in a panic. In my frantic attempt to become one with the bed, I miss the rest of Aunt Lisa's conversation with my future murderer. So I don't understand how it happens, but instead of the sound of her shoving him down the stairs, I hear a lock turn as Aunt Lisa opens the front door.

Footsteps—two sets.

Aunt Lisa's voice again: "I think she's asleep, but I'll check."

More than fear, I feel betrayal. I've known Aunt Lisa for less than a day, but we're family! How could she sell me out so quickly?

"Maisie?" A shadow leans over my bed. I go as still as possible, willing myself to become a pillow, for a pillow to become me . . .

"She's done in from the flight," Aunt Lisa says. "Jet lag and all. I don't want to wake her."

I breathe for the first time in twenty seconds, because "sleep-ing" is a much more realistic excuse for hiding from a stranger than *I am now a pillow*. I'm tempted to let out a few fake snores, but I don't want bad acting skills to give me away.

"I can come back tomorrow," the man says. "I didn't mean to barge in so late—you know how Edinburgh traffic can be."

"Hon, there's no need to apologize. Why don't you stay over? The settee folds into a bed—"

"The company put me in a hotel on Princes Street. I'll come back in the morning."

The Company? That sounds sinister. Who is this dude? Why did Aunt Lisa call him hon?

Aunt Lisa shuffles toward the door, blocking some of the light from the hallway. "Nonsense. I know it's cramped, but—"

"I don't want to intrude."

"Calum, you could never intrude."

Calum? I throw off my blankets and sit up straight in the same motion, staring at the stranger in front of me.

When Calum was sixteen and I was six, people said we'd look like twins if I were older or he were younger. We both had brown kind-of-wavy-but-definitely-not-curly hair, big cheeks and eyebrows, and "our father's nose"—whatever that means. As we grew, his hair got darker and mine got lighter. His face and body sharpened; mine freckled and curved. We still kind of have the same eyebrows, and I guess noses don't change. But there's no way anyone would say twelve-year-old me and twenty-two-year-old Calum look like siblings—not even if you tilt your head and squint.

By the way he's staring, I have a feeling we're thinking the same thing. "Maisie?" he mutters, like he can't believe I'm the same sister he abandoned six years ago, that this is the body I've grown into.

For some reason, my name in his mouth makes me angry.

He didn't warn me before he ran away, which makes sense. I guess. There's such a big age gap between us that it's not like we were close. But there's this thing with siblings. I see it in movies all the time. Siblings might not be friends—they might downright hate each other—but they always team up when it matters. To take down bullies. To stand up to their parents. I tried not to get angry at Calum for leaving and instead went for what Alicia calls "Indifference to His Existence." But, still. Why didn't Calum warn me before he ran away?

"Don't you live in London?" I press my back as far against the bed frame as it will go. Now that I'm not covered by blankets, I clearly see his wrinkle-free suit and shiny black briefcase. The outfit doesn't just look wrong because of the years it adds to his image, but because whenever I pictured an older version of Calum, I pictured Dad: baggy T-shirt, paint-spattered jeans, soft smile.

Calum taps the briefcase against his knee. "I have business in Edinburgh this weekend. I heard you would be here, so I thought I'd stop by." Even his voice sounds wrong. His words are formal and carefully chosen. A faint British accent clings to them, and I can't tell if it's genuine or put on.

"How did you know I'd be in Scotland?"

"Mom posted on Facebook."

That takes me aback. I never looked Calum up online, so I assumed he never looked me up, either. Why would he keep tabs on our family if he ran away?

"I actually swung round because I want to propose something." His gaze darts away from mine before bouncing back again.

I raise my eyebrows, because "propose"? Is he trying to impress me with his vocabulary skills? He sounds like Alicia, but at least she has an excuse for sometimes using pretentious words. She's a poet.

Aunt Lisa frowns. Calum obviously hasn't told her why he's here yet, either.

I don't say anything, so he continues. "I know you're meant to be staying in Edinburgh, but how would you feel about spending the summer in London with me instead?"

For a moment I just sit there, taking in the blankness of his expression, the blandness in his eyes. He's more similar to a robot than someone with a beating heart. Maybe that's why it's so hard for me to process his words.

"You. Want to spend the summer. With me?" I say it slowly, to confirm this isn't some weird misunderstanding.

He nods. "You're my sister. I'd like to get to know you."

I narrow my eyes. Calum had six years to reach out to me. If he wanted to spend time in person, he could have come home for the holidays. Or—here's an idea—he could have called me. On my *phone?*

"Maisie has plans already," Aunt Lisa says, placing a gentle hand on Calum's elbow. "She's to work in my shop. I don't think London is a—"

"What would I even do in London? I can't be old enough to work at . . . whatever fancy business place you need that briefcase for."

"You can't intern at my company, but there's plenty to do in London. You won't be bored."

I turn to Aunt Lisa. Her lips are pursed, and when we lock eyes, her frown deepens. "Your parents won't like this. They were anxious enough about sending you alone to Edinburgh. And Calum, I know you're an adult, but you're a young adult with a full-time job and no experience looking after children—"

"I'm not a child," I say quickly.

At the same time, Calum says, "I know what I'm doing."

Aunt Lisa sighs, turning back to me. "This warrants a discussion with your parents, but . . . if you're keen on going, I won't be the one to stop you."

"I . . ." It's almost midnight and my first day in a new country, and I'm jet-lagged, and my long-lost brother wants to spend the summer with me, and Aunt Lisa looks sad that I might not spend the summer with *her*, and—

"No," I say firmly. "Calum, I obviously don't want to spend the summer with you. It's hilarious you'd ever think I would."

He blinks once, hard, as though I clapped my hands in front of his face. "Right. Well . . ." He fishes into his pocket and hands me a business card. "My number's on here. If you change your mind, I'm in Edinburgh until Sunday night." His eyes flit back to mine and then away again. "I was hoping to finally meet you properly, but I understand. I'll—just go, then."

Meet, he said, as though we're strangers. *Meet*, like he wasn't at the hospital when I was born, like he didn't used to play Barbies with me before he realized he was a teenager. My anger flares, but . . . there's something about Calum. He's robotic, sure. But his words don't match his blank expression. I hear something in them that could be disappointment.

Now I'm the one who looks away. If he really wants to get to know me, why did he wait so long to reach out? How can I be sure this isn't some weird joke? I give him my best glower. "Bye."

Calum runs a hand through his hair, then gives another sharp nod. He and Aunt Lisa walk out of my room, closing the door behind them. I flop onto the bed and close my eyes, but my head is spinning too fast for sleep.

I Hate Ice Cream (Not Really, But I'm Trying to Make a Point)

I smell breakfast before I see it. Aunt Lisa stands in the kitchen making pancakes, an apron covered in cats wearing sunglasses tied behind her back. They're the kind of pancakes Mom makes—more like crepes than fluffy clouds—and it only now occurs to me this is probably a British thing and not a Mom creation. Aunt Lisa hands me a plate, and we sit at the small table in her kitchen.

"I rang your mum last night," she says, pouring milk into her coffee, "and we both agreed you should stay in Edinburgh. Calum's an adult, but only just. Besides, he won't be able to look after you with his work schedule."

"I don't need a babysitter." I don't know why I'm arguing. Aunt Lisa's right: I don't want to be alone in a huge city with a brother who doesn't even have time to text me *Happy Birthday* once a year. But last night, Aunt Lisa said the decision was mine.

"This isn't about you so much as it's about Calum," she says while shoving an entire pancake into her mouth. "I'd trust him with anything, but he's always been . . . erratic."

I frown. "You know him? Well?"

"He lived with me for two years before moving to London for university. You're sleeping in his old room."

My pancake shivers on my fork. "He lived with you? Do Mom and Dad know?"

"Of course."

Oh. I thought Calum just up and left; I didn't realize he went to live with family. Well—other family.

"Why did he run away?" I ask. There's an ache in my stomach. It started last night, and no matter how much water I chug, it won't go away.

Aunt Lisa is suddenly very focused on her own plate. "It took two months of asking before Calum told me his favorite food. You can imagine we never talked about anything much deeper."

I frown. "But you said you'd trust him with anything, which must mean you think he's a good person. How do you know he's a good person if you don't even know why he came to Scotland?"

Aunt Lisa grins. "He cleaned the toilet every few weeks. Voluntarily. What bad person volunteers to clean the toilet?"

My eyes roll before I can stop them. At the same time . . . she has a point.

Aunt Lisa sets down her fork while I devour my final pancake. "I open shop in two hours. Why don't you go and get dressed, and then I'll show you the ropes?"

From her casual topic change, I have a feeling she thinks this conversation about London is over. But I'm not ready to let this die just yet. If I stay in Edinburgh, it won't be because someone made the decision for me.

●●●

Ice cream shops look like fun places to work.

They're not.

Back home, I spend most of my time in the workshop with Dad. We don't talk while we're in the middle of projects, so I'm used to a quiet environment. I'm also used to working without an audience. Mom and Dad don't think I'm old enough to sit in on meetings with clients, so I base my sketches purely off their photos. In Aunt Lisa's store, there's a lot more pressure to perform well when a customer is watching you accidentally put hot fudge on their Goldfish Sundae instead of caramel.

A girl not much older than me walks into the shop and points at the ice cream display. "Chokorētoaisukurīmu onegaishimasu," she says. I think she's speaking Japanese, but I can't tell if she's pointing at Orange Cat or Grasshopper Mint.

I look around for Aunt Lisa. She's not by the cash register, so she's either in the storeroom or in the bathroom.

"This one?" I point at Orange Cat.

The girl shakes her head, so I start to scoop Grasshopper into a cup. But the girl shakes her head again and points—at Strawberry Butterfly?

Frustrated tears push at my eyes as the girl points again. "*Chokorētoaisukurīmu* onegaishimasu."

I point at Daydreaming Elephant. The girl holds out a hand, pulling up her phone. She types something and then turns the screen so I can see the Google Translation. チョコレートアイスクリーム = *Chocolate ice cream*. Oh. It even sounds similar to English; I can't believe I missed that. I dunk the scooper into Chocolate Sheep, serving the girl as fast as I can. When she walks out of the shop, I sink below the counter and press my face into my knees.

My phone buzzes. I grab for it immediately.

June 28, 1:35 p.m.

Alicia: You saw your brother?!?!

It's a response to my stream of messages from last night. On a normal day, I'd text her back immediately. But I don't really want to think about my brother when I'm already pushing back tears. Instead of replying, I scroll up, rereading some of our old messages.

February 13, 2:29 p.m.

Alicia: I figured out the perfect name for The Book.
Alicia: Dark Flower.

Me: But that has nothing to do with anything.

Alicia: I know, but doesn't it sound cool? Like a code name? People will buy The Book so they can figure out what it means.

Me: Maybe, but they'll be upset when they realize there's literally nothing in The Book about a dark flower.

Alicia: I can write a poem about a dark flower. I'll do it now. And you can draw a whole page of dark flowers.

Me: But that won't connect to anything else in The Book.

Alicia: Nothing in The Book connects to anything else in The Book!

Me: That's why we need to revise!! I'll come over in an hour so we can start.

Alicia: Fine. But I still really think we should call it Dark Flower.

Me: I really think we should not.

I won't cry I won't cry I won't—

Every minute I'm in Edinburgh is a minute I could be using to revise The Book or to convince Dad to give me more responsibility at Glenna's. I redo my ponytail and shake out my arms. The ice cream shop is empty; I should probably take advantage of the lull to clean the counter or refill the sprinkles.

Instead, I call home. I know I said I would grin and bear it for the summer if it meant Mom would stop bothering me about "finding other passions," but then I saw Calum. New things aren't exciting like Mom said they would be. I need familiarity. I need home.

"Piseag, I was about to ring you," Mom says when I bring the phone to my ear. "I told Dad not to post the news to Facebook until I got hold of you, but this time change makes things difficult."

My stomach drops to my toes. Someone must have died. That's always what adults mean when they have "news." I hope it's not Mrs. Thomson, the head of Crescent Valley's knitting club and our neighbor. I love doing my homework in her kitchen—there are always at least two cats vying for a position on my lap. "What news?" I say shakily.

"Oh, I thought you knew. Well, I'll just say it. You know how Glenna's is largely funded by Knightley Corporations? Since your grandmother's days, the shop has managed to thrive thanks to their investments. Unfortunately, we just got word that starting in August, Knightley will no longer be investing in small businesses."

It's a good thing I'm already sitting, because my legs turn to jelly. I brace a hand against the tiles so I don't dissolve entirely into the floor.

The thing is: We've had disasters surrounding Glenna's before. It kind of comes with the territory when you own a family-run portrait shop. But this . . .

This is different. Bigger. Without the funding we receive from Knightley every year, Glenna's is in big trouble. Our shop, my favorite place, my one true passion . . .

My phone almost slips from my grip because I'm squeezing it so tightly. "Let me come home. Please. I want to help—"

"No, no, we've got it under control. Dad and I started a petition and already have twenty signatures. We're researching grants and other corporations—don't worry, Piseag. We'll get this sorted in no time."

She's lying to make me feel better. She has to be, because there's no way a disaster like this can be *sorted in no time*. "Please," I urge. "I don't only want to go home because we lost the investment. I'm not happy in Edinburgh. I—"

"Piseag, you've only been in Scotland for one day! Give it a—"

"I don't *need* to give it a chance. It's not where I'm meant to be!"

Mom's impatience crackles through the phone. "I don't have time for you to complain about this, Maisie. Enjoy your summer. Remember that as boring or annoying as it is, it's going to be better than what we're dealing with at home."

My eyes narrow as something clicks in my head. "Did you . . . know we were going to lose the investment? Is that why you sent me to Scotland? Because you *knew*?"

I expect her to deny it. But after a thick pause, she says, "Over the last year, Knightley has been pulling their money out of small shops and putting it into what they've deemed to be more practical investments. We figured it would happen sooner rather than later."

Thunder builds in my chest. "So you sent me away because you didn't want me to be a burden—"

"Maisie, don't blow this out of proportion. I sent you abroad because I wanted you to enjoy your summer without having to worry about this."

"Why would you even want to spend money on plane tickets right now? If the shop is in trouble—"

"That's all the more reason why you shouldn't be complaining about this trip abroad! You are very lucky to have an aunt who lives in Scotland and is willing to house you for free. You should be grateful that, thanks to Grandma Glenna, we can afford to fly you across the ocean right now. It's a privilege to spend the summer having new adventures while we're managing a crisis at—"

I hang up. She'll probably call back in a minute to yell at me for being rude, and a guilty part of my brain knows I kind of deserve it. It *is* a privilege to be here—especially while Glenna's is in trouble. But Mom and Dad only bought that ticket to get me out of the way. They lied to me—*Dad* lied to me—about all that *Finding Your Passions* nonsense because they think I'm more of a burden than an asset to the shop.

Anger tunnels my vision. This is just like the time our basement flooded and Mom forced me to sleep at Mrs. Thompson's house for a week while "we handle this." Or when Calum jumped off our swing set and broke his arm and Mom made me spend the night at Mrs. Thompson's *again* because "we need to focus on your brother."

My brother.

I jump to my feet. Calum ran away from home-slash-Glenna's. He probably doesn't care about the shop, but not caring isn't the same thing as hating. If I can convince him to buy me a plane ticket home so I can petition with Mom and Dad, I can . . . maybe I can start offering art commissions on Instagram to save up the money to pay him back.

I stare at my phone. Calum gave me his number. I could call him right now, but . . . I'm still in the dark about why he left Crescent Valley. I remember lots of yelling. It could have been all that puberty stuff we've talked about in health class, but I don't know of any other teens who left the country because of hormones. My brother was never into art like the rest of our family is, so maybe he ran away because Mom and Dad were pressuring him to be more involved in the business. Whatever the reason, I need to be careful. Mom is stubborn. She won't change her mind about me coming home. Dad only sometimes takes my side, so he's too risky of an option. And Aunt Lisa clearly agrees that I should stay in Edinburgh.

Calum is my best chance. I don't want to ruin my best chance because I didn't do enough research.

My phone rings. Mom.

Instead of answering, I text Alicia:

1:47 p.m.

Me: I need your internet-stalking skills.

Alicia: My skills are at your service.
Who do you want me to creep on?!

Me: My brother.

I Thought My Brother Was a Literal Demon, But Maybe He's Just a Nerd?

The internet stalking takes place at 6:00 p.m. my time and 1:00 p.m. Alicia's time. Stale daylight streams through my curtains while fresh afternoon sun blazes across Alicia's bedroom in Crescent Valley.

"Calum Clark," Alicia mutters over FaceTime, presumably typing my brother's name into Google. "What have you been up to all these years?"

Alicia is a sleuthing genius, but I don't exactly need her skills to find my brother's public Facebook account. I roped her into this because I already miss the soft blue rug in her room, where we used to spend hours every week working on The Book. I miss her German shepherds, German and Shepherd, and the way her freckled face gets all serious when she's working out a problem. I see it through my phone: nose scrunched, ginger hair pulled into a messy bun, flush coloring her forehead and cheeks. Her mouse clicks away at links, so I turn my attention back to my own laptop.

I type "Calum Clark" into the browser. Results surface immediately. At first, it doesn't seem like he has social media aside from Facebook, but it's possible he has Twitter or Instagram under a different name.

"Did you see this?" Alicia asks, and sends me a link. It's a profile page for my brother at the fancy corporation he works at. And the corporation is—no freaking *way*.

"Calum works at Knightley?" I gasp, my eyes scanning quickly over his job description. *Assistant to Ms. Andrea McKinley, Head of Finance.*

Alicia stops clicking on links and looks up at me. "What's Knightley?"

"The corporation that stopped investing in Glenna's. Is this . . . is it just a weird coincidence?" Calum's profile is pretty bare, just an unsmiling photo and what looks like a work email address. There's nothing about when or how he got the job.

"Maybe your parents have a connection to the company?" Alicia suggests.

"I guess . . ." It's possible. But Calum isn't in contact with our parents. At least, I don't think he is, so it seems unlikely he would have used their connections to get hired. I click on his Facebook page. Maybe his social media will answer some of my questions.

And . . . wow. His page is public, but that's probably because he's got the most impersonal profile I've ever seen. His Facebook looks the same as his business page—he even uses the same picture. It doesn't seem like he's posted anything new in four years, but he's been tagged in a lot of photos. The latest collection, posted by someone named Benjamin Saito, includes ten pictures of Calum. But for all I know, they could be the same image with a green screen behind them. My brother stands the same way in each photo: hands in his pockets, shoulders hunched inward, eyes piercing the camera like he's trying to set it on fire. He's not smiling, and he's wearing a suit in all of them—even though the last picture was taken in a park. The Calum I remember was not the most expressive person in the world, but this is just ridiculous.

I tap on his profile picture, then swipe left to his earliest photo. It's from eight years ago, and the image catches me off guard. Calum at fourteen looks a lot like me at twelve. Maybe it's his expression. He's smiling in this picture, kicking his legs into the sky as he prepares to jump off the swing set in our backyard. There's something about the way his cheeks puff and his nose crinkles that reminds me of my own face.

I flip to the next photo, and oh. Two years later and it's Calum with Aunt Lisa. They're sitting on a bed—the bed I'm sitting on *now*. Aunt Lisa wears the same cat apron she had on this morning. Calum is rolling his eyes at her like he doesn't want to be in the photo, but there's a faint smile on his lips, like he maybe doesn't mind after all. The next picture shows him standing outside the massive Edinburgh castle I saw when I got off the bus yesterday. Then there's a time jump, and I'm back on his current photo. In eight years, he's only uploaded three pictures.

So, Facebook isn't very helpful.

"It's possible Calum has a secret Twitter or Instagram, but it might take me a while to find them," Alicia says. "Your brother is either really paranoid or really boring."

I close out of Google, frustration stiffening my fingers. I'll just have to be upfront with him about the plane ticket and hope for the best. "If he doesn't want to help me get home . . ."

Alicia lies on her rug and raises her phone over her head. "There might be another option."

"Yeah?" I say dully.

"Calum works at the company that stopped funding your shop. If your parents won't let you save Glenna's from home, maybe you and Calum can save it from London?"

I sit up so quickly that I almost hit my head on the bed frame. Calum probably has more connections to Knightley than Mom and Dad do. After all, he *works* there. If anyone can convince the corporation to reinvest in Glenna's, it's him. But . . .

There are a lot of buts.

"I still don't know why Calum left home. What if it's because he hates Glenna's? He was sixteen, so maybe Mom and Dad were pressuring him to show more interest in—"

Alicia waves a hand like she's trying to swat my mouth shut from across the ocean. "That's a problem for later. Calum invited you to spend the summer with him. He said he wanted to get to know you, so I'm sure he'll explain why he left home. If the reason has nothing to do with Glenna's, you can ask him to help save the shop. If he *did* leave because of Glenna's . . . well. We'll figure something out."

It's a good plan. It would be flawless if anyone else were involved, but this is Calum. I was surprised by the disappointment on his face when I said I didn't want to spend the summer with him yesterday, but that doesn't mean I suddenly trust him. What if I go to London and he ditches me on the side of a road somewhere? It sounds ridiculous, but I literally know nothing about him.

My phone buzzes. I do a double take when I glance at the screen. "Hang on, I think he just texted. It's an unknown number."

Alicia springs forward until her nose is practically pressed against her phone. "Read it out loud!"

Unknown: Hello, I hope you are well.

Alicia groans. "He sounds like an eighty-year-old. Who starts texts with 'hello'?"

I glower at her. "Do you want me to read it or not?"

She makes a show of zipping her lips with a finger and throwing the key behind her shoulder. I turn my attention back to my phone.

Unknown: Hello, I hope you are well. Lisa gave me your number because I wanted to reach out again before I leave Edinburgh. This is Calum, by the way. In case that wasn't clear.

Unknown: Maybe I shouldn't have randomly shown up at Lisa's in the middle of the night, but the truth is, I've been meaning to reach out for a while. When I heard you were in the UK, it seemed like a good time.

Unknown: If you don't respond to this message, I'll assume it's because you want nothing to do with me and I won't bother you again. But at least consider

> London. If nothing else, it's a nice
> city.
> —Calum

"He sounds kind of desperate to hang out with you," Alicia says when I finish reading.

I shrug. "Maybe that will make it easier to convince him to help me." I don't add that this text makes me even more confused about my brother. When he first left home, I used to draw him a lot. I thought the only type of person who could abandon their family would have fangs and red eyes and a forked tail (I was six years old, okay?), so I always made sure he never looked human. I obviously know now that my brother isn't a literal demon, but sometimes when I picture him in my head, I still see those red eyes left over from when I was young. Maybe it's time to throw that version of Calum away, though, because demons don't text their sisters weird rambling messages about how they've been "meaning to reach out for a while."

Unless they do.

Because it's a trap.

Is this a trap? My heart, which had been beating faster in my chest, suddenly squeezes. My face must change, because Alicia frowns and says, "What's wrong?"

I can't quite look at her. "Maybe Calum only wants me to come to London because he knows it will cause chaos. Mom and Dad wanted me to spend the summer with Aunt Lisa, so this could start a huge fight. What if . . ." I close my mouth. I'm not about to say out loud that the thought of my brother letting me down again is terrifying. When he ran away, I wondered if it was maybe because I'd done something to make him hate me. If I let myself trust him …

When I sneak a glance at my phone, I can tell Alicia gets it. She gives a small, sad smile. I wish I could hug her. I wish I weren't alone in a different country with a bunch of strangers who are supposed to be my family but who aren't actually my family because I don't know anything about them. The distance swims across my vision. I close my eyes, but it's still there.

"This is going to sound bad, but maybe it's okay if he's trying to start a fight?" Alicia says tentatively. "Not that I think Calum is lying, but … the reason you want to go to London isn't to get to know him, right? You'll be using him to save Glenna's. So would it really matter if he's using you for something, too?"

Wow. Yes. For a second, I let emotions get the better of me, but this was never about bonding with Calum. Alicia's right: The only reason I'm even considering my brother's offer is because I need to save Glenna's. This is not a family reunion. It's a business opportunity and nothing more.

"Keep him at a distance," Alicia continues. "That way, it won't hurt if he disappoints you."

"Please. The last thing I want is to get close to him." Before I lose my nerve, I open my phone and text him:

> 7:18 p.m.
> Me: I'll come with you to London. Don't tell Aunt Lisa.
> Me: Btw this is Maisie.

It's like Aunt Lisa hears my treason, because it's been over an hour since I holed up in my room, and she chooses this exact moment to barge through the door. Privacy, much? My stomach lurches and my cheeks heat, betraying my guilt.

"I've got to go," I whisper to Alicia, ending the FaceTime call and trying not to look suspicious.

Aunt Lisa eyes the way I'm sprawled like a potato across my bed. "You must still be done in from the flight, but you've not seen much of Edinburgh besides the shop and my flat," she says. "If you'd like, there's a wee hill we can hike that gives a brilliant view of the city."

My lips curl around a massive NO. View or no view, I don't want to climb a hill. Then again, if I really do run away to London tonight, this is my last day in Edinburgh. It would be a shame not to experience any of it. Especially if there are more massive castles.

"Okay." I look for my sneakers before realizing I haven't unpacked them yet.

"Do you want help putting your clothes in the wardrobe?" Aunt Lisa asks as I step toward my suitcase.

"No, it's fine." I can't look at her. "I'll unpack tomorrow."

"It will only take a moment—"

I quickly cram my feet into my sandals by the bed, then walk past her and out of my room in the hopes she'll follow. If she unpacks for me now, I'll have to repack everything tonight. "Isn't it getting dark?" I say quickly. "If we want to climb that hill, we should probably get going."

"Sunset isn't for a few hours." Aunt Lisa frowns, but after a pause, she heads out of my room and into the kitchen. She hands me a water bottle, and we walk out the door and into the fading light.

Hills Are Evil

Aunt Lisa is either an Olympian or a liar, because Arthur's Seat is not a "wee hill."

The climb is pretty; I'll give her that. The mountain is covered in yellow flowers that make my fingers itch for my sketchpad. Stone ruins scatter the path, and dogs run up and down the rocks with so much ease that I'm jealous they aren't sweating buckets like I am.

Aunt Lisa doesn't make conversation as we climb—thank God. I'm doing everything I can not to look like the biggest wimp on the planet, but if I open my mouth right now, the only thing that will come out is a massive ARGGHHHH.

When we reach the top of Arthur's Seat, I collapse on a rock and chug water like I've been stranded in the ocean for a month. While I die, Aunt Lisa does sit-ups.

Sit-ups.

Until now, I've struggled to find any similarities between her and Mom. But Mom is one of those weirdos who wake at 5:30 every morning to run ten miles, and I have a feeling this is a trait she shares with her sister.

Even though it's pretty late in the evening, the sky is still bright. I snap a picture of the greenery on my phone, but it doesn't come close to capturing the real view. Aunt Lisa rises and points toward the other end of the rock face. "Let's head over there. The weather's a bit dreich, but you should still be able to see the city."

I follow her carefully, trying not to fall to a painful death off the mountain. When we reach the other side, I forget how horrific the climb was. The city sprawls before us, all stones and spires, and I can even see a hint of the huge castle in the distance. Clouds float past at eye level, so close that I try to poke one. Seagulls cry around me; one lands on a rock less than three feet from my sneakers, and we lock eyes.

"Smile!"

I turn to see Aunt Lisa holding up her phone. I raise my arms above my head, pop a hip, and grin.

"Cute. I'll send it to you and your mum." She sits down, so close to the edge of the cliff that she could dangle her legs over the side if she unfurled them.

I hesitate, then sit next to her.

We don't say anything for several minutes; the scenery talks for us. Finally, Aunt Lisa sighs and tilts her whole body to the sky, arching her back like a cat. I wouldn't be surprised if she was one in a past life.

"I don't come up here enough," she says. "I used to run this path every morning during university. With your mum, actually."

So, I was right about the exercise passion. But that's not the thing I'm the most curious about right now. "How many years apart are you?"

"Just one. But I never let her forget I was older," Aunt Lisa says with a wicked grin.

Mom is a younger sister. I knew this was something we shared, but it's easy to forget when she so rarely mentions Aunt Lisa. There are photos hung in our house from when she and Mom were young, but considering she's Mom's only living family, shouldn't I have met her before this summer?

"Did you get in a fight or something? Is that why Mom moved to New York?"

Aunt Lisa twists a strand of escaped hair between her fingers, then tucks it into her bun. "We did fight. But that's not why she stayed in the States. She couldn't have known she'd meet your dad and fall in love."

"Oh." I glance sideways, trying to judge whether to ask my next question. Aunt Lisa looks pretty relaxed, so I go for it. "Why did you and Mom fight?"

Aunt Lisa wipes at a dirt stain on her snail-patterned dress. She sighs and then says, "When we were wee, Fiona and I spent all our time helping our mum run Glenna's. I was the artistic one; Fiona preferred researching clients and keeping track of the funding. We never stepped on each other's toes, and because of that, we worked well together. I think your mum assumed when we graduated university, we'd take over the shop as a team. When I told her I didn't want to work for Glenna's anymore, it caused a row."

This throws me. I can't imagine not wanting to work for Glenna's. It's been my dream job since before I knew what dreams were. "You didn't want to run the shop? Why?"

Aunt Lisa shrugs, looking out at the gray city beneath us. "I always wanted to open my own business. Start something that was truly mine, you know?"

I frown. Although the New York branch of Glenna's is technically a different shop than the one my grandmother started in Edinburgh, the heart of it lives on in the name and products. To me, that's one of the best things about Glenna's: getting to be a part of something that existed before I did. I feel a similar way about The Book. As messy as that collection of drawings and poetry is, I love that it's a combination of me and Alicia. It wouldn't exist without both our contributions, and I think that's really cool.

My sandals darken as the sky fades from gray blue to reddish purple. Fiery streaks paint the horizon; I can't tear my eyes away. "A few days ago, Dad said I should never let Glenna's become all I am, and Mom was going on about how I need to find new passions." I turn fully to look at Aunt Lisa. "But why do I need new passions when I already have one? And isn't it *good* to throw all of yourself into the thing you love?"

"Why do you love working for Glenna's?" Aunt Lisa asks.

I open my mouth, expecting the answer to slide off my tongue. When it doesn't, my stomach jolts. I love Glenna's, but I've never really thought about *why*. Is it because I like working with my family? Because I like painting? I can paint in another job, and I don't have to work with my family to be close to them. The legacy aspect of Glenna's is important to me, but it doesn't feel like a strong enough reason to explain the passion I feel for the business. Like, if we ran a restaurant instead, I'm not sure I'd be as in love with it.

"I don't know," I admit after a pause.

"Well, you have plenty of time to figure that out."

"Not really. Did you hear we lost our biggest investor?"

Aunt Lisa nods. "Aye, but your mum'll figure something out. She always does."

I wish I believed her. If I believed her, I'd cancel my plans with Calum and spend the rest of the summer at the top of this hill surrounded by sunset. It's just . . . if I don't try to save the shop and we end up losing it . . .

Aunt Lisa rises to her feet. "We should head back before the sun sets entirely. But I'd love to add this hike into my routine again. We can come back tomorrow if you'd fancy."

I smile. It makes my insides squirm. Maybe Mom was right—maybe I can learn to love Edinburgh. I already really like Aunt Lisa.

But Mom's real goal in sending me away wasn't so I could find new passions—it was because she thought I'd be a nuisance when Knightley's stopped funding Glenna's. I might not know exactly why I love our shop, but I do know it's my favorite place in the world and that I need to do everything I can to save it. If that means leaving this gorgeous city behind to spend the summer with a brother I want nothing to do with . . . so be it.

•••

I wasn't connected to Wi-Fi during our walk, so I didn't get any texts. But as soon as we return to Aunt Lisa's apartment, my phone buzzes. Calum.

I pull up the message chain I have with my brother:

Me: I'm coming with you to London. Don't tell Aunt Lisa.

Me: Btw this is Maisie.

Calum: Why shouldn't I tell Lisa?

Me: She wants me to stay in Edinburgh.

Calum: Okay.

Calum: Why did you change your mind about London?

Me: You were right. We're in the same country for the first time in years. That probably won't happen again for a while.

Calum: Okay.

Calum: Be ready to leave at half eleven. I'll text when I'm outside.

Me: Half eleven?

Me: Is that 10:30? Or 11:30?

Me: Hello?! I don't speak British.

Calum: Sorry. 11:30.

Goodbye, Ice Cream

Calum texts right on time.

June 20, 11:30 p.m.

Calum: I'm downstairs.

I'm in pajamas because it's late and I can't be bothered with real clothes, but my pockets are stuffed with my phone and wallet. Everything is packed except for my sandals and coat, which I slip on as I tiptoe toward the bedroom door. The lights in the living room are off, but I'm not sure if Aunt Lisa is asleep. My heart jumps to my throat as I wheel my bag across the fluffy carpet, thanking Aunt Lisa's decor choices for muffling my movements. How will I explain this to her if she catches me sneaking out?

I'm not running away! I'm just taking my suitcase for a walk!

I've decided I don't believe in material things anymore, so I'm throwing my clothes in the trash.

My shirts are haunted. I'm scared to sleep with them in my room.

Honestly, knowing Aunt Lisa's personality, she might believe all of the above. If she doesn't . . . I cringe at the look of disappointment that will inevitably show in her eyes. And even worse, she'll probably be hurt.

You've only been here a day and you want to leave?

I hear movement from Aunt Lisa's room. Adrenaline bursts through my body: I slide the note explaining where I'm going onto the kitchen table. Then I run to the front door and unbolt it as quietly as I can.

It's not quiet enough.

Maybe I'm imagining it, but the sound booms across the apartment—so loud I'm certain my parents can hear it all the way in New York. I drag my suitcase through the threshold and it catches on the top step, smacking into the metal with a hollow *dink*. I shut the door, more worried about speed than stealth at this point. It takes forever to get down the steps. Seriously, eons pass between the first stair and the last. Once I'm on the ground, I rush to the back door of the shop and undo the locks. As soon as it opens and fresh air hits my face, my muscles relax.

Success.

A car flashes its headlights at me, and my body tenses up again. Running away from Aunt Lisa was the easy part. Convincing Calum to help me save Glenna's? I don't even know if that's possible.

"It's a seven-hour drive from here to London," Calum says as I climb into the passenger seat of his shiny black car. "I'll get us to Newcastle for now, and we can finish the ride tomorrow." He glances back at Unique Sweets. For a second, I think guilt flashes across his face. Does he feel bad about stealing me away from Aunt Lisa? That's unexpected. Then again, Aunt Lisa called him hon last night. My brother looks more like a fancy ice sculpture than someone you'd casually call hon, so maybe he cares more about her than I assumed.

Calum pulls onto the road, and all I see in the dim light are his sharp profile and my jumpy knees. This is the first time I've been alone with him in six years. What do I say? It feels risky to even breathe.

"I . . . your car is nice." I prod the white dashboard with my toe.

"It's a rental, but thanks." Silence falls. Then abruptly he says, "Oh. I got you something. In the back."

I lower my leg to the ground and reach behind me, grabbing a shiny black bag full of blue tissue paper. I reach my hand in. When I pull it out . . .

It's a Barbie. Calum got me a *Barbie*.

When I look at him, his eyebrows are raised expectantly, like I should be thrilled by the doll in my lap. I don't want to hurt his feelings, but how old does he think I am? "It's . . . nice," I manage after a pause.

"You don't like it."

"I do . . ." I trail off, because there's only so much enthusiasm I can fake for a Barbie. "I just . . . haven't really played with dolls since I was eight. But it's really—"

Calum shakes his head. "You don't have to pretend. I'm not . . . I don't know what twelve-year-old girls like. I just remember when we were younger, you had a doll with a similar purple dress that you used to carry everywhere."

He remembers Arabella? That should make me happy. After all, Calum must have been thinking about me these past six years—at least a little—if he remembers the color of the dress my favorite doll wore. But if he remembers my favorite doll's dress, surely he also remembers my birthday. I didn't need him to call me. A text would have been fine. One comment on my Instagram. Just . . . *something*.

Take things slow, Alicia said.

Slow is good. But I at least need to know what I'm getting myself into. I decide to test the waters. "Did you hear Glenna's Portraits lost its biggest investor?" I ask hesitantly.

"Yes." Calum's eyes are back on the road. His face is neutral.

I prod further. "Does it bother you we might have to close the shop?"

Silence. That lasts way too long. I pretend to look out the window, but really I'm watching him from the corner of my eye. He's still expressionless, and I don't think he's going to respond, but suddenly he says, "I work in finance at Knightley Corporations, not investing. If you decided to come to London because you think I can save the shop—"

"What? No," I backtrack, trying to cover my panic. How did he figure it out so fast? I look down at my knees, steadying my voice. "That's not it at all. I don't even care about Glenna's. I was just—I was making conversation."

When I decided to come to London, I assumed I might have to stretch the truth a little. But to outright lie?

It's not about bonding, it's not about bonding, it's not about—

Calum's eyes flick back to me. "You really don't care about Glenna's? The last I remember, you loved it."

"When I was six, sure. But now I know how suffocating it is to work with Mom and Dad." It's hard to say the words. They're so against everything I believe. But it seems like I said the right thing, because Calum fully turns his head in my direction, as though he has this urge to suddenly *see* me.

Except . . . this isn't me.

I ignore the bitter taste in my mouth. Calum is my brother, but he's also a stranger. I don't owe him anything.

It's not about bonding, it's not about—

I gather my emotions into a ball and hurl them at the car window. The glass doesn't shatter for obvious reasons, but I do feel a little better.

●●●

We stay overnight in a small hotel in the center of Newcastle. In the morning, we eat a quick breakfast and head back to the car. As I'm buckling my seat belt, Calum's phone rings.

"It's Aunt Lisa," he says. He swipes the power-off button and the screen goes black.

"Shouldn't we tell her I'm safe?"

"You left a note. She knows you're okay."

I bite my cheek.

"Trust me, she'll give up after twenty minutes."

I have a brief moment of *is he trying to kidnap me?* before remembering Calum has experience in the running away area.

"Did it really only take Mom and Dad twenty minutes to stop calling when you left home?"

He starts the car. "I don't want to talk about me."

I scowl. He's the one who reached out, but now he won't talk about himself? Seriously? I try to hold my tongue. I can't.

"You completely disappeared six years ago, and now you show up and say you want to get to know me, but you won't answer any of my questions—"

"Please." Calum's voice cracks slightly. I pause. Although we talked a bit in the car last night, his expressions remained neutral verging on cold. I assumed that meant he just didn't feel things strongly, but from the way he's looking hard at the road and gripping the steering wheel with enough force to turn his knuckles white . . .

Maybe it's the opposite. Maybe he has a lot of feelings, and he doesn't like them to show.

"I'm not very good at this," he mutters after glancing at my face. "I'm sorry." He looks back at the road. "I'll answer any questions you have, so long as you don't ask about home or Mom and Dad or Glenna's."

I breathe out in frustration. Those are literally the only questions I have for him. I don't care about his life in London or what his hobbies are. He had forever to reach out about *my* interests but never did.

Before I can say that out loud, Calum asks, "How's school? Is Alicia still your best friend?"

"School's fine." I try to control my annoyance, but it's not fair that he gets to learn about me when he won't talk about himself. Maybe that's why I build on my lies from last night instead of telling the truth. "My favorite subject is . . . math. I love numbers and fractions and all that fun stuff. My least favorite subject is art. Drawing is so boring."

Calum's eyes widen marginally. "Really? You were so good at it when we were younger. And I don't much keep up with Facebook, but didn't you win some art award a few weeks ago? Dad posted about it."

"Oh, that was nothing. Just some contest my teacher at school submitted my work to. She didn't even tell me she was doing it." Another lie. At the end of last year, our entire school had an art competition. Over four hundred people from kindergarten through twelfth grade entered, and my painting of two kids playing at the beach won. It's the first time in ten years a student in middle school won. I've never been prouder of anything in my life, and now Calum thinks it was nothing.

An ache is starting at my temple. I lean my head against the window and change the subject. "You graduated from college recently. What did you major in?"

Calum hesitates, then seems to decide this isn't too personal of a question to answer. "Business." He presses on the gas as our lane clears out, and the green fields blur into blobs. "I joined an art society as well. Didn't click with it, but it wasn't the worst."

I almost fall over even though I'm already sitting down. "You did *art*?" I watch him carefully. "I thought you hated it. I mean, there's only one painting of yours at home."

He taps a finger against the steering wheel. "I don't hate it. It's just not my passion."

"And *business* is?"

"I don't know why you're so skeptical. You like math."

"I—" Oh. Right. That was a thing I said. I backtrack. "You joined an art society at school, but you didn't do art at home. So . . .

does that mean you left home because you hate Glenna's?" Alicia's "take it slow" advice has officially gone out the window.

Calum sighs. "I *just* asked you not to—"

"How is that a personal question? It's a simple yes or no. Did you leave home because you hate Glenna's? Blink once if you hate Glenna's."

"Maisie—"

I throw up my hands. "You're impossible!"

He glances sideways at me. "*I'm* impossible?"

"Yes." I break off into grumpy silence. Maybe this was a mistake. If Calum won't even tell me if he hates Glenna's, how am I supposed to convince him to help me save the shop? It's not too late. I could pick up Aunt Lisa's calls and spend the rest of the summer in Edinburgh, hoping my parents figure out the investment problem on their own. Except I can't get that conversation with Aunt Lisa out of my head.

Why do you love Glenna's?

If the shop goes bankrupt, I might never figure out the answer to that question. I can't give up on what feels like the most important question in the world because I'm scared of making Calum angry. "You owe me an explanation," I say.

He raises an eyebrow. "Owe you?"

"Yeah." I pack as much confidence into the word as I can. "Do you know how it felt when Mom and Dad sat me down on that awful sapphire couch and said, 'By the way, your brother is gone'? I didn't get it at first. I thought you'd left for summer camp or something. And then you didn't come back for the school year, and I was so confused. I kept waiting and waiting, but . . ." I trail off. I didn't mean for it to sound like I'm still upset. It was weird and confusing when he ran away, but I'm over it. I have been for years.

I clear my throat and continue. "I agreed to give you another chance to get to know me. Even though I didn't have to. But if you won't even tell me why you ran away, I'll go back to Aunt Lisa's and—"

"Fine." Calum looks slightly pained, as though I'm jabbing him in the side as opposed to asking a simple question. "If I'd been home when I graduated high school, I knew Mom and Dad would have guilted me into working for Glenna's. I didn't want to live in the same town and work for the same shop for the rest of my life. Is that enough of an answer for you?"

No, I want to say, because if that's the only reason he left home, why did he feel so uncomfortable opening up to me? He's definitely hiding things. I want to shake him until his secrets spill out. Instead, I sigh dramatically and stare out the window.

Calum merges onto the highway and we leave Newcastle behind. As we pass a road sign marking our location, I suddenly realize Newcastle isn't in Scotland. We must have crossed over the English border last night. I went from never leaving the state of New York to visiting two countries in a weekend. Despite everything, a thrill runs through me. Maybe there is some truth to Calum's words. I never saw the value in leaving home—everything I need is in Crescent Valley. But exploring new places is actually pretty cool. As stressed as I am about the investment and as annoyed as I am that Mom sent me here to get me out of the way, it's getting harder and harder to complain about this trip abroad.

Apparently I Sleep on the Floor Now

It's almost midnight when we reach London. We ate dinner at a rest stop, where I drank something called Ribena that Calum insisted I try. It tasted like strong Vitamin Water, and I have no idea what flavor "black currant" is supposed to be, but it's pretty good. While we ate, I resisted the urge to check my phone by asking Calum a ton of questions. True to his word, he answered everything so long as I stayed away from his Off-Limit Topics. I'm glad I finally know a little more about him, but his answers . . . well . . .

Some of the highlights:

1. His favorite way to relax = doing taxes. (What?!)

2. His favorite color = gray because it's inoffensive. (I strongly disagree. Gray is offensively bland.)

3. The type of music he likes = none. He prefers silence. (I repeat: What?!)

4. Does he have a girlfriend = I'm not talking about my love life with my sister. (Come on!)

5. Does he like animals = no, they're unpredictable. (EXCUSE ME THEY ARE CUTE AND FLUFFY.)

I mean this with all my heart: I think my brother is the most boring person on the planet. I tell him this, just to make sure he knows. He doesn't talk to me for the rest of the drive.

•••

I didn't expect Calum to live with anyone. He seems like the type of person who talks business at work and then goes home to an empty apartment, where he connects himself to a charging cord and reboots for the next day. But when Calum unlocks the door and steps inside, we're greeted by a white girl and an Asian guy.

"Oh, Calum," the girl says, looking me up and down. "I've had my suspicions, what with your ridiculous work hours and frequent 'conferences' in other countries. But kidnapping children?" She glances at the guy standing next to her. "Do I finally get my twenty quid?"

He winks. "We've been over this, Rose. All bets are off until he outright admits he's a spy."

I whip my head up to look at Calum. "You're a *spy*?" Suddenly it all makes sense. My brother's refusal to talk about his life, his closed-off expressions and body language, his lack of online presence . . . "Does Aunt Lisa know?"

"Now look what you've done. She actually believes you." Calum drops his briefcase on the coffee table. "This is Maisie. My sister."

"She believes us because it's *true*." The guy turns to me. "Are you really his sister, or is this part of his cover? You can tell us. We're trustworthy."

"The most trustworthy." Rose places a hand over her heart.

"I—" I glance at my brother again. He rolls his eyes hard enough that the story shatters. His roommates are just messing around, but honestly? Finding out Calum's a spy would be more believable than most of the things that have happened in the past few days.

Rose sighs. "I suppose you can keep your money, Benji. For now."

"Are you done?" Calum glowers at them both. "I need to finish some work before tomorrow." He turns to me. "Do you mind hanging with my flatmates for the rest of the night?"

He's going to leave me alone? I try not to let my fear show as I nod. This is fine. These aren't strangers—well, they are, but I doubt they're murderers or anything if they live with my brother. And maybe they'll be willing to answer my questions about him, seeing as he's decidedly not a secret agent.

"How long will she be here?" Rose asks. "No offense." She turns to me and offers an apologetic grimace. "It's just, we don't have much space."

The apartment is pretty cramped. It didn't occur to me that leaving Aunt Lisa's would mean giving up my breathing room. "I'm here until August," I say hesitantly.

"*August?* Calum, you couldn't have given a bit of warning? Where is she going to *sleep?*" The girl glances at the guy—Benji—who is standing by the coffee table. Then she throws back her head and sighs. "She'll be in my room, won't she?"

I glance at Calum in alarm. "Wait, what? Why can't I sleep in your room?"

He narrows his eyes at the wall. "I leave for work at six every morning; I wouldn't want to wake you. Besides, all of my work is spread on the floor . . ."

The girl waves a hand, more dramatically than necessary. "It's fine. So long as she doesn't mind the air mattress."

I bite my lip. I've never had to share a room with anyone before, let alone someone I don't know. And this girl doesn't seem super happy that I'll be invading her space. But I knew this trip wouldn't be easy. I'm just going to have to be brave.

"Let's get you sorted." The girl grabs my suitcase and gestures me toward the hallway. I follow as she turns into the second door on the left, trying to keep my nerve.

It's a nice room. There's a decent amount of floor for me to lie on, but it's definitely not ideal. A queen-sized bed dominates the space, and posters of boy and girl bands line the walls. The fact that I don't recognize any of their faces is another reminder of how much older Calum and his roommates are than me. I don't belong here. Not even a little.

The girl turns to me. "Sorry about this. I suppose Calum didn't mention our living situation before you agreed to stay over."

"He didn't."

The girl grins, like she can read the discomfort in my tone. "It's not as cramped as it looks. Besides, the three of us are hardly ever home at the same time. Calum's always at work, and Benji and I are in a master's program at the University of London, so our schedules are a bit erratic. I'm Rose, by the way. Sorry about earlier—I don't mind you staying in my room. I was just surprised."

She talks very fast and gives a lot of information at once, so I ignore the details and just focus on her. She seems outgoing, which is good because I'm pretty intimidated by the fact that everyone here is so adult. But Rose doesn't look intimidating. Weirdly, she looks a bit like Alicia. She's short—almost as short as me—and has big blue eyes, freckles, and a wide smile. Her dark, curly hair is in a bouncy bun on top of her head, and she's wearing an oversized sweatshirt with University of London printed across the front, black leggings, and fuzzy pink socks.

Even *I'm* more intimidating than those socks.

I begin to relax as Rose grabs an inflatable mattress from the back of her closet and rolls it open on the floor.

"So," she says, "what are you planning to do while you're in London?"

"Maisie loves math, so I was hoping she could shadow you," Calum says from the doorway. How long has he been standing there? My brother really would make a good spy. I'm only ninety percent convinced he isn't one.

Rose glances at me. "I'll have to check with my professor to see if you can sit in on lessons, but are you sure you want to? It's summer. No one wants to do maths in summer."

"You do." Calum rolls his eyes, but not in a mean way. "You're literally taking summer courses." He turns to me. "I know it's not ideal, but like I said in Edinburgh, I can't take you to work with me. I promise I'll keep my evenings free, though. Is that all right?"

There is negative zero part of me that wants to spend my summer in math classes. I open my mouth to protest, then quickly snap it shut again. As I discovered in the car, Calum is super closed off. If I'm too demanding, he might get annoyed, and then he won't help me with Glenna's. Worst-case scenario, he could even send me back to Aunt Lisa. So I nod, and ohmygod. I can't believe I'm agreeing to do *math*.

●●●

After my bed is set up on Rose's floor and I've come to terms with living out of a suitcase for the next few weeks, I turn off airplane mode on my phone and plug in the Wi-Fi code Rose gave me. At first, there's nothing. My heart sinks. I don't want my parents to freak out at me for leaving Scotland, but it would really suck if they didn't call once.

My phone connects to the server. After a delay, the messages come in at full force—so fast my eyes blur.

Eighty-five missed calls. Forty texts. Most of the texts are from home, but fifty of the calls are from Aunt Lisa. There are also a bunch of messages from Alicia.

And . . . now I feel terrible. I shouldn't have listened to Calum. I should have answered on the first call to keep everyone from worrying. Texts are still coming in, and I'm sure they're the opposite of rainbows and sunshine. I tap open my messages like I'm holding a bomb.

Monday, June 21, 10:06 a.m.

Mom: Lisa just rang. You're going to London with Calum????

10:07 a.m.

Mom: I tried calling. Please answer.

10:09 a.m.

Mom: Maisie, turn your phone on.

11:12 a.m.

Mom: You are not an adult.
Mom: You can't run off and cut contact
    with me.

11:22 a.m.

Mom: This is serious.

12:10 p.m.

Mom: Maisie, answer your phone.

10:30 a.m.

Dad: Can you call me or Mom? We're very
    worried.

12:15 p.m.

Dad: I'm sure you're okay but we'd really
    like you to check in.

1:05 p.m.

Dad: Pick up your phone, Maisie.

2:45 p.m.

Alicia: H
Alicia: E
Alicia: L
Alicia: L
Alicia: O
Alicia: Are you in London with
    Calum or not?!?!

3:49 p.m.

Alicia: I'm going to take your
silence as a yes.
Alicia: But maybe confirm you're alive? Your
parents texted to see if I've heard from
you. They're freaking out.

I close my eyes and try to steel my nerves. This is going to be brutal.

•••

"I know," I whisper for the eight thousandth time, trying not to let this conversation leave Rose's room. "I shouldn't have left Edinburgh without telling you. I should have kept my phone on. I'm sorry."

"Sorry isn't good enough!" Mom's voice booms so loudly from my phone that I have to hold it away from my ear. She told me we're on speaker, but Dad hasn't said anything in the twenty minutes we've been on the call. I suppose I should be grateful only one parent is exploding in my ear.

Of course, just as I think this, Dad says softly, "Why did you go with Calum? What was your thought process?"

At least he's not damaging my eardrums.

"I don't know," I stall, because I can't tell them why I really followed Calum to London. If I do, Mom will yell at me for butting in on adult things and might tell Aunt Lisa to bring me back to Scotland. "He's my brother. And . . . I haven't seen him in six years. And . . . I want to get to know him."

Silence on the line. One second. Two. I've either said something meaningful that is causing Mom to reevaluate her anger, or she can smell my lies from across the ocean and is about to start shouting again.

I lay it on thicker. "I never thought Calum would reach out to me. I thought he wanted nothing to do with me. So when he said he wants to spend time together . . . I know it was wrong to leave Aunt Lisa, but I just . . . I want to get to know my brother." I attempt a small sob, and it actually doesn't sound fake over the phone. My acting skills level up by a hundred when I'm not looking my parents in the face.

"Oh, Piseag." Mom's voice goes all scratchy. "I didn't know you felt that way."

I pause. I didn't think I felt that way, either, but now that the words are in the air, they feel less like a lie than they did in my head. I didn't come to London for Calum—I'm here for my family, the family that didn't run away without looking back. But if Mom told me right now that she found a way to save Glenna's Portraits and the business was up and running again . . . don't get me wrong, I still don't trust my brother. But I also don't think I'd be ready to leave.

The anger fades from Mom's voice. "You scared us, Maisie."

"I know." As annoyed as I am that my parents won't let me come home to help them with Glenna's, I hate hearing that frantic edge to Mom's tone. I don't like it when she and Dad are upset. Especially not when I'm the reason behind it. "I'm sorry," I say more sincerely this time. "I won't do it again."

"Good." There's silence for a moment, but it doesn't feel heavy like it did at the start of the call. Finally, Mom says, "I need to know what you'll be doing in London. You have to keep in contact with me. Phone calls every day. Twice a day. And—"

My heart soars. "Does this mean I can stay?"

"You need to apologize to your Aunt Lisa. I also need to know who will be looking after you while Calum's at work, and that you won't be traveling around the city on your own. If I like your answers, then . . . yes. I suppose you can stay. But," Mom continues before I can get a word in, "turning off your phone was extremely irresponsible. If you do *anything* like that again, the consequences will be severe. Do you understand?"

"I understand." I can't quite keep the excitement out of my voice. In this moment, ominous threats and strange brothers and sleeping on the floor don't matter. I get to stay.

I get to *stay*.

Math Class in the Summer?!
No Thank You

Alicia: The Tennis-ing has begun.

Alicia: They make me RUN.

Alicia: EVERY DAY.

Alicia: I'm so SWEATY.

Alicia: ALL THE TIME.

> Me: Ew I'm so sorry.
>
> Me: But also, I'm about to do MATH.
>
> Me: Can we trade places?

Alicia: Yes, please.

The only good thing about sitting through a math lecture during the summer is that it's not *my* lecture. The teacher can't come up to me at the end of class and say *Why were you staring at the ceiling?* or *Here's your homework—you got a D.* The only person I need to impress with my math skills is Calum, and he's not even here.

Well, I guess I also have to impress Rose and Benji. If they figure out I don't actually *loooove algebra, oh my God it's my favorite thing ever,* and it gets back to Calum, I'll have some explaining to do. But hey, it is kind of cool to sit in on a master's-level class. I might not be a teenager for another 101 days, but this definitely makes me feel grown up.

I file into the room with Rose on my right and Benji on my left. The class isn't like anything I've seen before. At home, there are about twenty kids in my grade, and we're split into two sections of ten. Meanwhile, there are fifty people in this *room*. It's circular, with whiteboards at the front and rows of chairs with small desks attached.

"How many people go to this school?" I whisper as Rose edges into a row of seats toward the middle of the room.

"There are only forty-seven students in our program, but there's got to at least be one hundred fifty thousand enrolled at the university."

I blink, sure I misheard. *One hundred fifty thousand?* That's more people than Crescent Valley, the town next to Crescent Valley, and basically every other town within a half-hour drive from my house combined. I knew London was bigger than Edinburgh, but if one hundred fifty thousand people go to this one school, how many people live in this city?

I have the sudden urge to crawl under a desk.

Instead, I take the seat between Rose and Benji and try to make myself look bigger. People are definitely staring. I don't know why it didn't occur to me that I would stand out.

Benji nods his head in my direction. "I think you're a little old for this class."

I frown, but then he smiles, and some of my tension melts. Even though I had to take a twenty-minute subway ride (or *tube* ride, according to Rose) with Benji this morning, I'm still not sure what to make of him. Unlike Rose, who wears her emotions front and center on her face, Benji's are more relaxed, like he's not too bothered about whether or not they show. His outward appearance is similar to his casual atmosphere. His dark hair is messy, but in a way that looks deliberate. His black jeans and jacket are covered in paint, but not like mine are after a day in the workshop. There are designs in the splatters, and a detailed sunflower decorates the back. I've been wanting to tell him how much I like his jacket since I first saw it, but at breakfast and on the tube he seemed to be scrambling to finish a homework assignment.

Rose was chattier. We spent the commute talking about school and music and books—she mentioned she likes graphic novels, and I almost started fangirling before I remembered I'm pretending not to like art. There were a few spaces between conversations where I almost jumped in with questions about Calum, but I learned the hard way in the car that I've got to take this slow.

"We'll be picking up on page 139 of your textbook," the professor says.

Rose flips her book open, and when I glance at the page, my eyes bulge.

This isn't *math!?*

I know sometimes there are letters in math. We started doing algebra in school last year, so I know about x and y, but the symbols in Rose's book aren't even letters. Well, some of them are. But there are also massive backward *E*s, and I see an upside-down *A*, and there's something that looks like an *O* with a squiggle of hair on top.

I knew I would be out of my depth here, but what was Calum *thinking*? He must have known I wouldn't get anything out of this class—aside from nightmares of higher education.

"Before we move forward, I want to circle back to our discussion about imaginary numbers," the professor continues.

"What?" I say out loud, because this isn't the type of shock you can keep to yourself. I nudge Rose in the side. "Did she say *imaginary* numbers?"

Rose smiles and pulls out a spare sheet of paper. "It's impossible to take the square root of a negative number," she whispers, drawing a –1 inside a little house. "But if we *imagine* we can solve a negative square root . . ." She writes an equal sign and then a lowercase *i*. "Now we can solve equations that need the square root of a negative number! Isn't that brilliant?"

"No." My brain is exploding. "You can't . . . you can't just create fake numbers! Who decided that was allowed?"

Rose's smile widens, but then the teacher glances our way, and she ducks her head into her book.

I spend the next forty minutes drawing birds on the sheet of paper Rose left on my desk. I know this fake version of me is supposed to hate drawing and love math, but we all have coping mechanisms, and mine is covering –1s inside little houses with feathers and talons before they can hurt me.

When I draw, time doesn't fly. It skips. One second the clock reads 10:20. I tilt my head toward the page and my world fills with ink. When I come up for air, the clock reads 10:38. Head back to page. Eyes to clock. 11:01, and the students around me are packing up their bags.

"Those are excellent," Benji says as I fold the paper into a small square and slip it into my pocket. "I love the shading, and your page placement is perfect. Do you also do word art? You've got a steady-enough hand for it."

My eyebrows rise. "Are you an artist?"

"It's a hobby," Benji says as we file out of the classroom and into what looks like a student café. Rose has another math class in an hour that I'm supposed to shadow, but I'm not sure I can make it through a full day of learning about fake numbers.

Rose huffs. "I don't think you can call criminal activity a 'hobby.'"

My eyes widen. "Criminal activity?"

Before I can totally freak out, Benji interjects, "It's street art. Rose likes to be dramatic."

She crosses her arms. "Nothing is dramatic if it's illegal."

He grins. "It's only illegal if you get caught."

Rose makes a noise somewhere between a scoff and a snort. "Oh, wonderful. That's a fantastic thing to say in front of a twelve-year-old. Calum will be chuffed."

Benji raises an eyebrow. "You know perfectly well I go through the proper channels." He turns to me. "There are organizations that buy wall space for artists to paint on, and more shop owners than you'd expect commission murals for their buildings."

"You go through the proper channels *now*," Rose counters. "But when we were in uni—"

"Do you really want to start a conversation about our life choices in uni? Because I could easily bring up the Harry Styles pencil drawings you used to post to Instagram—"

Rose gasps. "I posted *one* drawing. One time."

"Once on your main account. As if I don't know about @harryforever53."

Rose looks scandalized. I step between them before their bickering can escalate. "Hold on. You both do art?"

Rose gives Benji one last glower and then shrugs. "I did a bit in uni, but not so much now. I was never as serious about it as Benji or Calum."

Apparently imaginary numbers aren't the most unrealistic thing I'm going to learn about today. My stomach jumps. I cross my arms to keep it from leaping out of my throat. "Calum? Does *art*?" He mentioned he did some in university, but that's different from being "serious about it." And didn't he say it wasn't his passion?

He lied to me. *Why?*

"Rose, Cal, and I met our first year of uni because we all joined the school's art society," Benji says. "Rose did pencil drawings for a while, and Cal writes and draws a web comic. He also collaborates with me sometimes when I do street art."

My face does a weird twitch thing when he says my brother's name, because first "art" and now "Cal"? Cal who does street art doesn't sound like the kind of guy who works in a fancy investment job. Cal who makes web comics doesn't sound like the kind of guy who runs away from his art-obsessed family.

I bite my cheek. I don't really remember how Calum spent his free time when he lived at home. There are soccer trophies in the living room, but I don't have memories of going to his games. I think he won a spelling bee, but that was probably Mom's fault.

It's possible he got more interested in art after he left home, but that would be kind of weird since we literally run an art business. You'd think he would have discovered his passion when he was surrounded by Glenna's.

I lived with Calum for six years, but I'm starting to realize just how little I know about him. And if I—his *sister*—know so little about him, how well do his flatmates know him? "You've known Calum for what? Four years?" I ask Benji. "But you looked surprised last night when he told you I'm his sister. Did you even know I existed until yesterday?"

Benji exchanges a hesitant glance with Rose. "He's . . . mentioned you," he says carefully.

That doesn't make me feel better. If Calum talked about me, why did he never talk *to* me? My jaw clenches. It's like I'm looking at a painting but the image is blacked out. I see color at the edges, the hint of a story. But I can't guess at the picture beneath because so much is covered.

I'm trying not to look upset, but I must do a bad job, because Benji hesitates again and then says, "I assume you stalked Cal online before coming here, so you must know he's quite private. But he actually does have an Instagram. There aren't any photos, and he only follows one person, but that person is you."

Shock runs up my body. I shiver from the jolt of it. "What?" I whip out my phone, my heart bouncing awkward patterns in my chest. "What's his handle?"

"@generic_usernameoooo."

"Of course it is," Rose says as I type it in.

Benji's right: When I search through my followers, I find the account. I keep my profile public because I sometimes post my Glenna's sketches for our customers to see, so it's pretty normal for me to get follows and likes from random people. I actually do think I've seen this handle in my notifications before, but I just assumed it was a bot because of the name and lack of photos.

If Calum follows me, it means he knows I lied in the car about hating art. Why didn't he call me out?

And why has he been stalking my Instagram instead of reaching out to me directly?

I chew on my lip. Benji and Rose exchange another glance. This one is more determined than the last. "You're done with class for the day, right?" Rose asks.

Benji nods.

"Why don't you take Maisie to Camden? Show her some of the art you and Calum did there."

Benji doesn't look thrilled by the idea, but I perk up. You can tell a lot about a person by their art. Sometimes it's obvious by the subject matter, but there's also a ton you can learn from the style, the themes. Dad has a light, flowy style. When he's not painting for Glenna's, he does word art and abstract designs that remind me of the clouds his head is always in. Mom doesn't do a lot of art, but when she does, it's all sharp edges and angles, black lines on a white background. I haven't really found my style yet. Sometimes my pencil is bold, other times it's airy. I draw a lot of birds, but I also do abstract. When I flip through my sketchbook, I see individual pictures—not a collection. I can't even guess at what Calum's art will look like. Robotic? Realistic? A bit lost, like mine?

Rose pulls out her phone. "I'll let Calum know the change of plans."

"No," I say quickly. I don't know much about my brother, but I'm sure the last thing he'd want is me prodding through his art. "Don't say anything. Not saying anything isn't the same thing as lying."

Benji purses his lips. "It definitely is the same thing."

"It's not," I press. "But even if it is, it's not like I'm going alone. He can't get mad if I'm with you, right?"

He hesitates. "I don't know . . ."

I jump up. "Glad we've figured this out. Let's go." Mom once told me that when she's dealing with a particularly difficult client, she takes charge of the situation even when she feels totally out of control. *Because,* she said, *when you act like you know what you're doing, people tend to believe you.* I'm a full decade younger than Benji and Rose and thousands of miles from home. But if I'm sometimes intimidated by adults because I can't understand them . . . maybe adults are intimidated by me, too.

Rose sighs and tucks her phone into her pocket. "I won't text him. But if he texts me, I'm telling him where you are."

I grin.

Benji Can't Keep Secrets

June 22, 2:34 p.m.

Alicia: So Rowan is in my tennis class.
Alicia: They're good at it, which is a
horrible turn of events. But even worse:
Alicia: They LIKE tennis?!?!
Alicia: I don't know if we can come back
from this.

Me: Oh nooooo.

I don't remember seeing street art in Edinburgh. Granted, I was only there for a day. But the cobblestones were bare, like nobody wanted to mess with the medieval fairy-tale vibe the city was going for. London is a different story. Art is plastered on brick walls, on stone. On sidewalks and storefronts and mailboxes. I love the chaos and the color.

Benji pulls out his phone as we hop on the tube. He's quieter than Rose, but he's not the kind of quiet that my brother is: blank and unyielding. Benji's silence takes up more space, in a way that lets me know he's listening, even as his fingers tap away at a game on his screen. I pull out my own phone before remembering I'm not supposed to be using data. Mom got me an international plan, but "it's for emergencies." Unless I get lost or hit by a bike or fall down a hole, I'm not allowed to use it off Wi-Fi.

"This is us," Benji says when the tube lady announces, *This is Camden Town.*

We hurry off the train and climb a few flights of stairs. When we emerge onto the street, I gape.

It's like we've stepped into a different universe.

There's art everywhere and like I've never seen it before. The buildings are all painted different colors: pink, yellow, blue, red. Most of them belong to storefronts, and they're covered in the most elaborate designs I've ever seen. There's a tattoo parlor with massive plastic flames attached above the awning. There's a tourist shop nestled under a painted dragon that looks 3D. There's even a shoe store with a giant yellow Converse sculpture mounted above the entrance. And when I say giant, I mean it's taller than me and Benji stacked on top of each other.

If my jaw drops any lower, it will hit the earth's core. "What is this place?" I whisper.

Benji smiles. "I thought you'd like it."

I do, but I also don't. Every square of cement is crammed with tourists. Yes, I'm aware I'm also a tourist. I have nothing against tourists, but they're *loud*, and walk so *slow*, and the heat of summer plus packed streets is not an equation I want to be a part of. Benji leads me down the long blocks while I try to pay attention to the art above me instead of the people around me. But when he says, "Keep your phone close," suddenly all I can think about are pickpockets, and how math class is horrible, but at least it won't kill me, and—

We turn off the main street. When the crowds fade into the background and the sun stops glowering in my face, I can breathe again. Benji taps his foot against a brick wall. It takes me a moment to realize the art plastered across it must be his and Calum's. I raise my gaze to take it in. And the image . . .

It's weird.

An old man sits in a chair. There's a window behind him, looking out on jagged mountains designed like fangs. In front of him is a dog—but it's also a devil, with horns and an arrow-tail and more fangs. Instead of features, across the old man's face are the words "No promises."

My stomach sinks. I had this feeling that when I saw Calum's art, I would instantly know his heart. But this piece . . . I have no idea what it's supposed to mean, let alone which lines were painted by him and which were done by Benji. They either have the same cartoonish style or are very good at working as a team. My art combined with Alicia's poems always looks like we're trying to jam together two puzzle pieces from different box sets. How did they create something so cohesive?

"It's a bit strange, I know." Benji smiles slightly. "But I don't do art for myself."

"What do you mean?"

"I approach people on the street and tell them I'll paint whatever they want. Sometimes they ask for dirty images or jokes, but a lot of times they'll ask for something really specific, like this." Benji traces the dog's tail with his finger.

I look more carefully at the image. "My family's business also creates customizable art. We mainly do portraits of people, but sometimes we take specific requests like pets or meaningful objects. Dad was even commissioned to illustrate an autobiographic children's book once." My eyes widen. When Aunt Lisa asked me why I love working for Glenna's, I didn't have an answer. But actually, I *do*. I want to work for Glenna's for the same reason Benji creates street art: to help people express themselves. What job on earth could be more important than that?

My shock fades into relief. I didn't just get swept away in Glenna's Portraits because it's been around me my whole life. Well, maybe my passion started because of that, but I have my own reasons, my own motivations, for wanting to keep Glenna's alive.

I turn back to Benji. "How did you first get into this? Does your family also do art?"

"Ha, no. Both my parents are lawyers. They would not be happy if they learned I've taken to . . . er . . . vandalizing the streets of London. Not that they'll find out—they moved back to Japan a few years ago." Benji backs away from the wall. "I drew a lot as a teenager, but didn't get into street art until university, when I met Cal. He had the idea for this project in our first year but wasn't very confident in making art outside of his web comic. He suggested we work on it together. That's how we got close—we started dating a few months later."

My eyes had been glued on the devil dog, but they snap to Benji so fast that they sting. "You *dated* Calum?"

"Dating. Present tense." Benji frowns, twirling his jacket cord around his finger. "He didn't tell you?"

"I thought we already established Calum doesn't tell me anything!"

"Oh." Benji shoves his hands into his pockets, breaking eye contact with me. "He said it was fine for me to bring it up in front of you. I assumed that meant you knew . . ." He trails off. "Can we pretend it was Rose?" He points a finger at me. "Rose told you. Not Benji. Rose. Got it?"

I frown. "Do you seriously think Calum will be upset? Dating isn't some adult thing I'm not allowed to know about. I'm twelve, not two. My best friend is in a relationship. I know a girl who's been dating the same guy since fourth grade."

"It's just . . . well." Benji fidgets with his jacket again. "Calum's a guy. I'm a guy . . ."

"Okay?" I grew up with Alicia, and with Mrs. and Mrs. Matthews, and with Mom and Dad telling me it's normal to have crushes on people of any gender. I've not had any crushes yet, but if I do get one, I really don't think I'll care if it's on a girl or a boy or someone nonbinary like Rowan. That's never seemed like a big deal to me, but I know not everyone grew up in Crescent Valley.

Benji's hands are clenched slightly, like he's ready to either block a punch or throw one. I put more caution than usual into my words. "I don't care who Calum dates. I'm just . . ." I look Benji up and down. His haircut is less fancy than Calum's, but it's cooler, with the sides short and the top long. And the style of his sunflower jacket is similar to the art on the wall, so I assume he hand-painted it. "Why would you want to date *Calum*?" I say finally. "No offense to my brother, but he's somehow both boring and a mess."

Benji's mouth twitches. "Calum's a bit closed off, but that doesn't mean he's boring. After all, he may or may not be a spy."

I shake my head. "You can't keep joking about that. I'm only eighty-five percent sure you're joking."

Benji's grin widens. "It checks out, doesn't it? Boring job that no one wants to ask about, constant business trips, the sealed document I found on his desk last week with huge red Top Secret letters stamped on the front—"

"Very funny."

Benji tries to give me a serious look, but his eyes are still laughing. "If you ever find out he actually is a spy, you must let me know. Even if they threaten to make you disappear. And by 'they,' I of course mean the expressionless men with sunglasses who force you to sign a nondisclosure agreement by lamplight." He holds out a hand. "Promise?"

I roll my eyes, partially because he's being ridiculous, but also because if expressionless men with sunglasses do threaten to make me disappear, I obviously won't spill anything.

"Secret agent thing aside, you can't deny Calum's a mess," I continue. "He spent years ignoring me and then randomly showed back up in my life without explaining why. He brought me to London even though he doesn't have time for me—or space! I'm sleeping on a floor! And unlike you, I *don't* want to take math classes in the summer. Especially not when they involve fake numbers."

"Didn't you tell Calum you like maths?"

I cross my arms. "That's beside the point. And not that you and Rose aren't nice, but I didn't come to London to hang out with you. I came here for my brother."

"Have you told him that?"

"I . . ." I guess I never said it explicitly, but I shouldn't have to. Like, I obviously didn't leave Edinburgh and Aunt Lisa to get to know Calum's roommates—well, roommate and boyfriend. I kick the wall behind me with the heel of my foot. "Why did he run away from home? If you're dating him, you obviously know. Don't pretend you don't."

Benji breaks eye contact with me. "It's not my place to talk about Cal's past. But you're right: He shouldn't have brought you here if he wasn't going to open up at least a little. I can nudge him on it, but he'll be more likely to listen if you talk to him, too."

I bite on my lip to keep from replying. It's hard to let my curiosity go, especially when I'm sure Benji knows more than he's saying. At the same time, I get how pushing him on this could put him in a weird position with Calum. I'd hate to give them relationship problems; if my brother is this closed off now, what was he like *without* a boyfriend?

"Want to head home?" Benji asks, nodding in the direction of the tube.

It's been a long day, and I have a feeling I'm in for an even longer conversation with Calum. I step away from his art. "Let's go."

My Brother Lied about Shrek

Calum gets home while Rose, Benji, and I are eating dinner. I pretend to be engrossed by my pasta, but really I'm watching my brother out of the corner of my eye. I may have completely missed the fact that he's dating Benji, but Calum is bound to slip up at some point. If I look for it, I bet I'll find proof of their relationship.

"How was your day?" Rose asks as Calum sets his briefcase by the door and takes off his fancy coat. "Crush any hopeful business owners' dreams?"

"You know that's not my job," he mutters. "How was the vortex of time and space? Still an infinite mass of nothingness?"

Rose is studying to be an astrophysicist, which sounds like the coolest job ever—and that's coming from me, a person who wants to throw the entire concept of math out the window. What I mean is: Calum's burn is pretty weak.

Rose sticks her tongue out at him. "I'm trying to convince my professor to name the new black hole she found 'Calum.' Quite fitting, don't you think?"

"Is someone going to ask about my day?" Benji asks before Calum can retort.

Rose leans closer to him and smiles sweetly. "Do anything fun after class? Some street art? Maybe in Camden?"

He kicks her under the table. "You know me, just maths. So much maths. Drowning in maths. Anyway—"

He cuts off when Calum walks over to the table and kisses him on the cheek. My eyebrows rise, because that was not the discreet evidence I'd been straining my eyes for. Rose lets out a sharp laugh and quickly covers it with a dramatic cough. Benji's eyes widen, but it takes Calum another five seconds to realize what he did. His back is to me, but suddenly he freezes. His head starts to turn in my direction, but he suddenly changes course, walks over to Rose, and pecks her on the cheek as well.

This time, she doesn't disguise her snort.

Calum straightens and slowly turns toward me. He's almost as red as my ruby jean shorts. "I . . . lost a bet? We were playing trivia." His eyes fall on Rose's water mug, which has a bunch of animated characters on it, including the girl from *Brave*, the horse from *Tangled*, and the donkey from—"*Shrek* trivia. We take game night very seriously in our house. Especially when it's . . . *Shrek*. We are very passionate about *Shrek*, because who wouldn't be, and anyway, it's quite annoying that I lost, but wasn't today the last day? I'm finally free from . . . having to kiss you both when I come home from work. Thank God. It was the worst."

"Liar." Rose's voice is muffled because she's covering her mouth with both hands. "You know perfectly well you've got two more years left. Never bet against me at *Shrek* trivia."

"Ah, yes." Benji's eyebrows are raised so high they almost touch his hairline. "Our . . . *Shrek* bet. I nearly forgot. How . . . absurd of me."

Rose cackles into her elbow. Benji bites down on his lip. Calum glowers at them both.

I open my mouth, because Calum can't actually think I believe this? Before I can say anything, he grabs my arm and yanks me up from the table. "We've got somewhere to be."

"We do?"

He nods.

"But—"

"It closes at half nine. If we want a full hour there, we have to go now."

This is 100 percent an excuse to get me away from a cackling Rose and a baffled-looking Benji, but I don't have a chance to protest before my brother pulls me out the door and onto the street.

Calum starts walking briskly. I have to run to keep up. Suddenly he starts babbling, as if this will keep me from getting a word in about what just happened in the flat.

"Did you have a good day? I had a good day. Well, it was a bit boring, because a meeting with a client fell through and my boss is on holiday, so all her work is going to me, and I had to read through a bunch of contracts, which isn't my favorite, but all in all nothing awful happened, and anyway, I know you want to learn more about me, so I think you'll like the place we're going, as it's a—"

I grab his wrist, yanking him to a full stop on the pavement. "I know you and Benji are dating."

"What?" he says in the worst fake-surprised voice I've ever heard. "You mean that thing in the kitchen? No. Like I said, I lost a bet—"

"You're an awful liar, and I really mean *awful*. A bet? A *Shrek* bet? Come on. I'm not three. Also, Benji told me."

Calum runs a hand through his hair. "He told you?"

I roll my eyes. "He thought I already knew. Probably because you told him he could talk about it with me? And because most brothers tell their sisters when they're dating someone instead of saying they *lost a* Shrek *bet*? Really, Calum. I hope you know I'm going to hold this over you."

"Please don't. Rose is already having a time with it." He shows me his phone screen. It keeps lighting up with new texts.

June 22, 8:03 p.m.

Rose: HA
Rose: HAHA
Rose: HAHAHA
Rose: HAHAHAHAHAAHAHAHA
HAHAHAHAHAHAHAHAHA
HAHAHAHAHAAHAHAHAHAHA

I'm glad I'm not the only one who thinks he's ridiculous. I let go of his arm and cross mine over my chest. "First I find out you have a secret Instagram account you use to stalk me with, and then you try to hide your relationship from me? I thought you wanted me to come to London so we can get to know each other. How am I supposed to get to know you if you keep lying?"

Calum blanches. "How on earth did you find out about the Instagram? Wait, don't tell me," he cuts in as I open my mouth. "It was—"

"Benji," I finish, and he groans.

"I really need to have a word with him."

I scowl. "Pretty sure you owe me a talk, first."

Calum hesitates. Then he grimaces. "I was going to tell you. It's just . . . sometimes, when people find out Benji and I are dating, they don't want to be around us anymore. There was a chance you might run back to Aunt Lisa before I got to know you properly. I . . . was going to tell you." The second time, it sounds more like a question than an explanation.

I frown at him. "I'm not some jerk stranger you met on the street." He still won't look at me, so I kick him in the ankle. "I like Benji. Though I'm not sure how you ended up dating someone so much less boring than you."

"Wow. Thanks."

I kick him again—in the other ankle this time. "Don't lie to me. That's the only thing that will send me running back to Aunt Lisa."

Calum runs a hand through his hair again. Finally, he looks at me. "You're kind of cool," he says after a pause. "For a twelve-year-old."

I push my shoulders back. "I've been told I'm very mature for my age."

"That must be why you keep kicking me."

I aim at his shins this time; he jumps away. "Come on," I say, and start walking again. "At this rate, we'll never get to whatever mystery location you're taking me to. Is there even a mystery location? Or were you just trying to get me out of the house?"

He's so much taller than me that he matches my pace in two long strides. "I said I'd keep my evenings open for you. I've had this planned for some time."

I try to keep my face neutral, but I didn't know he was actually planning stuff out for us to do. It's weird to imagine him sitting at the kitchen table, creating a list on a pad of paper of activities he thinks I might like. My steps are weightless as we walk to our destination, and there are several times where I have to stop myself from skipping. My excitement fades fifteen minutes later, though, when we stop outside of a three-story town house and I read the sign by the door.

"Museum of Finance?" It comes out as a whine. "You took me to a *finance* museum?"

"It's great," Calum says, and for whatever reason it sounds like he means it. "They've got a massive coin exhibit, and an entire room dedicated to the history of UK currency, and you'll learn about the finance markets—gosh, I'm getting giddy just thinking about it. I promise, you're going to love it."

"Love" is a strong word, but I try to return his smile as he leads me through the front door.

We're the only people here. The old woman tending the desk looks happy when we walk inside, and I'm not surprised. She probably hasn't seen anyone come through in hours—or, let's be real, days. Who in their right mind would spend their free time at a finance museum?

"Hello, Calum," the woman says, because of course she knows his name.

He waves at her, then leads me through the entryway and into the first exhibition room. Before I've even taken a breath, Calum points at a bunch of rusty coins and starts nerding off with more passion than I've ever heard from him. I try to pay attention because he's so excited, but it's just . . . the *worst*.

". . . and then we move into the fourteenth century . . ."

Sometimes when I'm bored, I draw things in my head. It sounds weird—how can you draw without supplies? But it's more like I memorize the shapes of the objects near me and move them around in my mind to form new images. I start with the glass cases of rusty coins, rotating them into a back corner of my mind and stretching the image to fill a whole room. If I were to walk into my imaginary exhibit, those rusty coins would tower over me.

I place Calum in my mind museum. And I make him tiny— the size of an ant. I picture him scrambling over the coins and spinning around the ones with gaps in their centers like a hamster on a wheel. I amuse myself with this for way too long, until finally—*finally*—we're exiting the building and walking onto the lamplit street.

"So," Calum says as we start toward home, "what was your favorite part? I love the bit where they talk about the formation of the financial markets."

"That was . . . interesting." I'm trying really hard not to sound like I had the worst time ever. He wanted me to enjoy this, and if we can bond over finance, maybe he'll help me save Glenna's. "I liked the coins. It's cool looking at . . . old things."

Calum turns his face away like he doesn't want me to see his smile. "After all the hassle you gave me over the *Shrek* bet, I thought you'd be a better liar. Admit it. You were miserable."

"What? No, there was . . . you know . . . money. And finance, and things . . ."

He waves my words away. "It's fine. I'm not quite as out of touch as I'm sure you think I am." This time, he doesn't hide his grin. "I knew you'd find it awful."

I snap my head up to glower at him. "You *knew* I'd hate it? Why would you take me somewhere you knew I'd hate?"

"For all the trouble you've given me for lying, you've been a hypocrite." Calum raises an eyebrow. "I know you lied about liking math. I hoped you'd get so bored with my rambling about financial markets and thousand-year-old currency that you'd come clean."

"I don't hate—"

"Benji said you spent the majority of his and Rose's lecture softly banging your head against your desk and muttering 'Lord take me now.' Besides, I had a feeling you were lying about math in the car when you also lied about not liking art."

Right. The whole "My Brother Has a Secret Boyfriend" thing kind of sidetracked me from the whole "My Brother Has a Secret Instagram That He Uses to Stalk Me With" thing. Now that we've cleared the first one up, I'd really like to yell at him about the second.

"Don't turn this back on me," I snap. "Yeah, I lied. But it was only because I wanted you to like me. What's your excuse for the Instagram? If you'd put in a profile picture and followed me like a normal person, we could have—I don't know—*talked*? Instead, I've spent the last few years thinking you couldn't care less about me. Why does everything you do have to be a secret?"

Calum rolls his eyes. "You just said you lied because you wanted me to like you. Did it not occur to you my reasoning might be the same?"

I frown. I went into this London adventure thinking I needed to convince Calum I'm worth having around. It didn't occur to me that he might be doing the same thing, but I've been forgetting something important. *He's* the one who left *me*. I'm not the one who has things to apologize for. He's probably unsure if I'll ever forgive him for running away.

"This is complicated," I say finally. "Our family is complicated, isn't it?" I don't add *it's complicated because of you*. It's the truth, but I don't want to hurt him. Even though he hurt me. I've never really admitted that to myself, but it hurt when he left. It was a stab to the chest, and the wound never healed over. Sometimes, when I'm around him now, it actually hurts more than when he was far away. I mean, I can't pretend he doesn't exist when he's standing right next to me.

Calum nods slowly. "Complicated is the word."

"You're still not going to tell me why you left home?" If he would just answer that one question, it would clear up so many things.

He looks away. "I haven't decided yet."

I groan. Whatever. If he's still going to keep secrets, I don't have to come clean about everything yet, either. I'll ask him for help with Glenna's eventually, but . . . this doesn't seem like the right time to tell him the real reason I'm in London.

"I'm sorry," he says quietly. "I know you're frustrated. There are things I want to tell you. It's just . . ."

"Complicated." The more I say the word, the more annoying it sounds.

"Sorry," he mutters again.

I don't get how there can be things he wants to tell me but that he also can't. I don't understand why everything has to be a puzzle with him. At the same time, Calum reached out to me. He brought me to London and cleared his evenings for me. I have to at least give him credit for that. I elbow him in the side. "After that nightmare museum, I think you owe me ice cream."

He lets out a startled laugh. "There's a place on our way home."

"Is it finance themed?"

"Do you want it to be?"

"You wish."

My Parents Hate Twitter

Alicia: One day of tennis felt like one year.
Alicia: I can't do this for an entire summer.
Alicia: Can I come to London and hide in
    your suitcase?!?!
Alicia: Also I haven't heard from you in a
    while.
Alicia: How are things?!?!?!

Me: Sorry I've been really busy.
Me: Can't talk now.
Me: But I'll fill you in soon!!

I wake early the next morning and spend a half hour on Google. When we went to Camden, Benji mentioned that Calum has a web comic. If I can find it, it might tell me everything I need to know about why he ran away from home. But my brother obviously isn't using his real name, and I don't know him well enough to guess his fake one. I try things like *FinanceandArt* and *MathWebcomic* until I get annoyed and start searching *WhyIsMyBrotherSoAnnoying* and *StopKeepingSecretsCalum!*

The truth is, I've been in a bad mood since last night. After we got back from the finance museum, I had the brilliant idea to follow Benji on Instagram to see if his page would reveal any new information about Calum. I had to request to follow his account, but when he accepted . . .

He has over two thousand followers. Rose and Calum appear in a lot of his photos, alongside a ton of other people who must be their friends. And in all of the pictures, Calum is casual with Benji like he only was that one time in the flat when he forgot I was there. An arm around Benji's shoulder, or hands tangled together, or an easy smile on his face that I've never seen in real life.

Calum hid his relationship from me, but he clearly doesn't hide it from his friends. That realization stung, but it only really hurt when I saw a photo of Benji and Calum and a woman at a café. Some of the captions on Benji's photos are in English, and others are written in Japanese. When I translated this one, it said: cappuccino + boyfriend + older sister = <3.

Benji has a sister. She was tagged in the photo, so she clearly knows they're dating. If it's not a secret from her, why did Calum hide it from *me*?

There's no point in asking—I know my brother well enough by now to know that. So I just sigh, flex my fingers, and continue failing to find his web comic on Google.

●●●

On Thursday, I get up early to look for Calum. I have a few non-finance-themed ideas for evening activities that I want to run by him.

"Sorry," Rose says, hopping into her bed with a cup of coffee when I return from my failed mission. "Cal's never around in the mornings. I saw him leaving for work at half four when I went to the toilet."

"Four? He went to work at *four a.m.*?" I plop back down on my floor bed and run quick fingers through my tangled hair. "Does he always leave that early?"

Rose shakes her head. "He usually goes in at six, but he's been leaving earlier to clear his evenings for you."

I didn't know he was doing that. I don't want him to leave for work at *four in the morning* because of me. "Does he even like his job?" I ask. "It seems so boring, and that's way too many hours to be working in a day."

Rose sips her coffee. "When I met Calum at uni, he was working three jobs. And almost every second he wasn't working, he was studying. He says he just likes to keep busy, but . . ." She shrugs.

"What?"

Rose sets her cup in her lap. "I met Calum in an art society. He was so passionate in those meetings that when he first told me he was concentrating in business, I thought he was joking. But art can be a risky career choice, and he doesn't have family to fall back on. Your aunt occasionally reaches out, but Calum won't take her money. He's been supporting himself financially since secondary school because he didn't want to be a burden while he lived with her."

My eyebrows pull together. I thought Calum was boring and overworking himself because it's his personality. It probably *is* his personality—at least to some extent. But it should have occurred to me that part of the reason he works so much isn't because he wants to.

"He always has his phone on him, though," Rose adds. "If you need to speak with him, I'm sure he'll pick up."

"Thanks." I don't want to bother him while he's at work, especially not when I don't have anything important to say. Speaking of phones, though, when I check mine, I have three new texts. One from Mom, one from Dad, and one from Aunt Lisa.

June 24, 4:30 a.m.

Mom: How are things going?

5:03 a.m.

Dad: Are you settling in okay?

7:57 a.m.

Aunt Lisa: Wanted to check in. You all right?

My stomach twists. I haven't talked to Aunt Lisa since I fled her apartment in the middle of the night. She's called a few times, but I haven't known what to say, so I let the messages go to voice mail. It's unfair to keep avoiding her, though, so I text back:

8:04 a.m.

> Me: Things are good! I'm very sorry I left Edinburgh. I really liked your ice cream shop and getting to know you. I'm sorry if I made you mad or upset. I hope we can meet up before I go home.

Then I send a group text to Mom and Dad.

> Me: London is nice. Calum and I went to a museum yesterday!

A few minutes later, my phone buzzes with a reply from Mom. Isn't it the middle of the night in New York? My stomach pangs. If I were home, Mom and Dad would have another pair of hands helping to find a new investor for Glenna's. If I were home, they'd be able to get more sleep.

> Mom: That's great! So glad you're having a good time.

> Dad: Not sure if Mom told you, but we started a petition for Glenna's and it's going well. We're going door to door, and we already have ninety signatures!

> Me: I'm not sure a petition is enough. I've been doing some research on shops that saved themselves, and most of them did it through social media. Have you tried making a Twitter account for Glenna's? Do you want me to make one?

> Dad: You don't need to worry yourself over that. We're making good progress from home!

> Mom: It's much harder to find help on the internet than it is to ask for it in person.

Me: That's not true at all. You can reach so many more people online than you can in real life.

Mom: Dad and I know what we're doing. Like he said, don't worry about Glenna's!! Have fun in London.

I must groan audibly, because Rose looks at me.

"Our family business is having trouble," I explain. "I told my parents to make social media for the store, but my mom thinks it's a waste of time."

Rose shakes her head. "My mum owns a bookshop and she's the same way. For years, she didn't even have a website. I finally did it for her, and a week later she called me, all 'Rosie, we've had so many sales this week!'" She rolls her eyes. "I could have screamed."

"Our business has a website, but I want my parents to make a Twitter."

Rose grabs her laptop off her nightstand. "Why don't we do it for them?"

I hesitate. If Mom finds the Twitter and gets mad that I'm interfering when she told me not to, she could decide to send me back to Aunt Lisa. But if I don't take any risks, we're going to lose Glenna's. Despite what Mom says, social media *is* our best bet at saving the shop. I walk to Rose's bed and sit on the edge as she pulls up Twitter. "Thanks for helping me."

She grins. "Of course! What are friends for?"

She probably only said that to be nice. I smile back anyway.

•••

Two hours later, and I can't believe I'm in another math class.

I spend the majority of the lesson checking the Glenna's Twitter on my phone. The shop only has four followers, and I think they're all bots because they don't have profile pictures. Still, it's better than zero. Although I'm off to a slow start, I have to admit this Twitter thing is kind of fun. Art is my one true passion, but I sort of understand why Mom enjoys working on the business side of Glenna's. When I draw, I'm creating something out of nothing. It's the same with this Twitter account. I'm creating an audience, an image, that didn't exist before. It's exciting.

An idea hits me like a bolt of lightning. Literally, it's so fast and strong I shiver in my seat. Benji looks over at me with mild concern. "You all right?" he whispers.

"I finally understand imaginary numbers!"

"Really?"

"Of course not."

He scoffs in a joking way before refocusing on the professor.

I lower my gaze to my desk. The real reason I went rigid is because I figured out how to save Glenna's. Mom's petition isn't going to work because it's just names on a list. A lot of names might be meaningful, but Mom and Dad aren't going to get close to the number they need by knocking on people's doors. Especially not when we lose our funding in a little over a month. In order to save the shop, we need to prove the work Glenna's does is valuable. I'm trying to prove that on Twitter, but audiences aren't built overnight.

However. What if I don't need a huge audience? What if I just need the *right* audience? My heartbeat increases as the plan forms more fully in my head. In order for this to work, I'm going to need Calum on my side, which is annoying. But before I need Calum, I need Benji.

"Hey." I corner Benji after the math lesson ends. "Are you planning on doing street art today?"

"I wasn't, but I could be convinced otherwise." We wave goodbye to Rose, who has a second class in ten minutes. "Why?"

"I think it's so cool that you use art to help people express themselves. I'd love to learn what your process is like." I make my eyes all big and wide, because I need him to say yes more than I need anything else right now.

Apparently I put more effort into that than I needed to. "All right," Benji says easily and nods toward the street. "I've been meaning to interview people by Westminster for a while. Want to head over now?"

I grin.

How to Make an Angry Old Lady Even Angrier

Alicia: Tennis was painful yesterday.

Alicia: Not just because it's tennis but also because a ball smacked me in the face.

Alicia: It was kind of awesome though because I got to sit out of class for twenty minutes.

Alicia: Anyway, are you around tonight? We haven't talked in forever.

Me: No, sorry.

Me: Still super busy.

Me: But I'll let you know when I'm free!

Benji and I hop on the tube. He pulls out his phone and starts playing a game, so I scroll through my photos from the past few days. It's weird to see Calum's face in my camera roll. Most of the pictures I have of him are candids, because he refuses to smile and pose when I point my phone at him. I did get one selfie of the two of us when he took me for ice cream after the finance museum. I'm grinning, and he looks annoyed that there's a camera in his face, but he didn't swat it away, probably because he was more concerned with shoving ice cream in his mouth. I laugh a little, looking at it. For a second, I consider posting it to Instagram. He wouldn't like that, though.

I make it my phone background instead.

I glance at Benji. He's still immersed in his own phone, so I start to turn back to mine. But then, because I've been holding on to this for a while, I say, "Your sister knows you and Calum are dating."

He looks up. "My—? Ah. You've been looking at my Instagram."

"You didn't have to accept my follow request!"

He smiles. "I know. That wasn't an accusation."

Oh. I'm so used to Calum shutting down when I ask questions that I forgot not everyone is like that. "Sorry," I mutter. "I just—why is he okay with her knowing? When . . ."

When he didn't want to tell me?

Benji slips his phone into his pocket and gives me his full attention. "During my first year of uni, my parents moved back to Japan to take care of my grandmother. My sister and I weren't close beforehand—she's five years older—but we were alone here once they'd gone. We started seeing each other more often, and Cal doesn't have family in London either, so my sister began inviting him over for holidays and such. They've been close a long time. Since before we started dating."

I hear what he's not saying: that Calum isn't close with *me*. This isn't new information, but it hurts to hear someone else acknowledge it. It makes it more real. And the thing is, I never wanted to get close to Calum. Caring about people is scary, especially when you aren't sure if they're going to care back. But . . .

I used to lie sometimes, when people asked if I had siblings. It was easier than explaining the truth. But now that I've spent time around my brother, he's not just a blurry memory anymore. I want to know what he likes and what he hates, and what he finds boring and what he finds funny. I want to care about him, even if he doesn't care back.

My face must be doing something weird, because Benji taps my foot with his. "It isn't a secret."

"What isn't?"

"Our relationship. Well, not everyone knows, but it surprised me he kept it from you."

"Oh." If that was supposed to make me feel better, it absolutely did not.

Benji smiles again, smaller. "What I mean is he doesn't normally hesitate. I've only seen him hesitate when he's telling someone who matters."

"Oh."

Benji's grin widens. He doesn't say anything else. I don't, either, so we sit in silence for the rest of the ride.

●●●

When the tube stops at Westminster Station, we get off and walk to the river. This is probably the most touristy part of the city—the massive clock tower, Big Ben, looms to the right; the London Eye, AKA that big Ferris wheel thing that's always in postcards, sits on the other side of the bridge we're approaching; there are dozens of red telephone boxes scattered across the streets, and tourists occupy every one, posing for cameras. Benji scours the area. I try to understand his thought process when it comes to choosing his next art piece. There are thousands of people on the street, so what makes him walk toward the old woman leaning against a lamppost?

She's tall, thin, and wearing all black—sort of like the lamp. She's not searching the street like the rest of the stopped people, who either scan for cameras or look for their wandering friends. This woman watches the world with glazed-over eyes, like she's not a part of it.

Benji takes a step toward her, but I grab his elbow. "Can I videotape your conversation?"

"All right. But why?"

I repeat my words from before. "I'm curious about your process." I don't say that while a petition or even a Twitter account might not be enough to convince funders Glenna's is important, it *might* be enough to go to the investment department at Calum's office with recorded evidence of how art can help people express themselves. If the department realizes how impactful art can be, they might consider reinvesting in us.

It's a ridiculous idea. I'm fully aware of that. But, hey. I'm desperate.

The old woman looks wary as we approach. She looks even warier when I ask if I can record her on my phone. "You'll be showing this to people?" she asks, her voice clear and crisp, the poshest British accent I've heard so far.

"Yes," I say. "If that's . . . you know. Okay." I'm pretty sure there are laws about recording people without their consent, so although lying would be easier than asking for permission, it's not a good idea.

The woman raises a skeptical eyebrow, but doesn't tell me to turn off my phone.

"I'm an artist." Benji nods at his sketchpad, which is tucked between his arm and his side. "I wanted to ask if there's anything you would like painted."

"No thank you," the woman says stiffly, turning away from us. "I don't much enjoy being solicited for money on the street—"

Benji steps in front of her. "It's free. I ask people what they would like painted—"

The woman crosses her arms. "Because you are lacking in your own ideas?"

My eyebrows rise. This lady has *sass*.

"I don't paint for me," Benji backtracks, "I do art for the people who can't—"

"So you have a savior complex?"

I consider stopping my recording. This conversation isn't helping my case for Glenna's. But Benji isn't budging, which means he must be used to this sort of backlash. He opens his sketchbook and holds it out for the woman to see. "I painted this for a man who finalized his divorce last week." He points at a pencil drawing of half a heart plunging toward the ocean floor. Then he nods at an image of a girl flying on a dragon. "She failed her pilot test for the third time." He flips the page, revealing a bundle of puppies. "This little boy just really liked dogs."

The old woman doesn't soften. If anything, she hardens more: her lips pursing and her eyes piercing through the sketchbook.

She considers Benji for a long moment. Finally, she says, "You're passionate about this."

He flinches, like he was expecting a jab instead of a pat on the back. "Yes."

The woman glances back at the sketchbook. "Passion is the devil's gift. Once it runs out—and believe me, it *will* run out—your life will lose meaning. Best not to have passion at all, in my opinion."

"Are you . . . were you an artist?" Benji asks.

"A writer. But one day you're packing up your typewriter to marry a lawyer, and the next you have six children and not even the energy to close your eyes at night. I'm dried up now. An empty vase." She taps the sketchbook with a manicured nail. "There's your inspiration. I won't even charge you for it."

The woman walks away, over the bridge in front of us, but Benji is already sketching. There are a million things I want to say, but this doesn't seem like a moment I should interrupt.

Benji finishes his drawing in under a minute and shoves his pencil into his pocket, gesturing me forward. "We can still catch her." He sprints across the bridge. I follow on his heels, panting as we dodge tourists and dogs. We catch up to the woman just as she crosses the river. Benji taps her on the shoulder, and when she spins around, she looks shocked to see us.

"How's this?" Benji asks, holding out his sketchbook once again.

The woman narrows her eyes at him, but she leans over his elbow. I inch around his other arm to see the drawing.

It's a rough sketch of a vase. A crack runs down the side, and the handle is splintered, like someone clipped it on a wall. But the vase isn't empty. A rose grows from the center, and it's not suspended in water like flowers normally are. It has roots sprouting from the bottom that dig into the cracks and crevices of the glass. This flower isn't going to wilt after a few days and get thrown in the trash.

"It's beautiful," I say before I can stop myself.

Benji writes an address on the edge of the paper and rips it off, holding it out to the woman. "I'll have it up by the end of the week."

She takes the address, slipping it into her purse. She doesn't say thank you, but the fire in her eyes has dimmed to an ember.

I stop recording and shove my phone into my pocket. I'm not sure if this video will be enough to convince Knightley Corporations to reinvest in Glenna's, but as we head back to the tube, Benji mentions he'll be collecting more stories tomorrow and I can join if I want. Hopefully, if we keep this up for a week, I'll have enough evidence to build a solid case.

Museums Don't Always Suck
(Then Again, Sometimes They Do)

June 28, 3:05 p.m.

Alicia: Are you around?

Alicia: I'll show you a tennis pic over FaceTime.

Alicia: It's super embarrassing so there's no way I'm texting it to you.

Alicia: But trust me when I say you'll be laughing about it for days.

6:45 p.m.

Me: I want to see!!!

Me: I promise I'll let you know as soon as I'm free to chat.

It's been a week, and Calum still hasn't admitted to me that he likes art. But on Friday, when I suggest going to a museum for our nightly activity, he agrees.

Museums can be super boring. You're supposed to stare at a bunch of stuff you aren't allowed to touch and read tiny captions about dead people. Even art, my one true love, can feel dry when you're looking at it from the confines of a spotless, air-conditioned building. However, there is also something really cool about getting up close and personal with a painting that was created four hundred years ago. It's probably as close as I'll ever get to traveling in time.

Calum takes me to a museum called the V&A, where we stare at paintings for a solid hour. Fun fact: Unlike in New York, a lot of museums in London are *free*. You can pop in, marvel at a few paintings, and leave without feeling like you lost money. Which is exactly what we do.

I focus mainly on the art, but occasionally I look over at Calum. When he catches my gaze, he rolls his eyes like he's just here for my benefit. But when I watch him from the corners of my vision, his eyes travel from the detail work of each piece to the layout to the background. I know he's analyzing the painting like I do, filing the imagery and techniques away for future inspiration. I may have only seen one of his street art designs and thoroughly failed to find his web comic, but Calum's an artist. It's obvious he loves it, which is why I finally decide to bring up Glenna's again.

Calum is staring at a framed picture of a stained-glass window. It's beautiful: colored with a kaleidoscope of blues and greens, the brushstrokes fading into each other until they all but disappear. I can almost see the sun shining through the panes, even though they're made of paint, not glass. I step beside him, watching him cautiously. There's no way to ease into this, so I don't try to. "You know how Benji approaches random people and asks them what they want painted on the streets? I've been going with him and filming those random people for a project."

Calum snaps his head toward me, the peaceful spell woven by the museum broken by a sentence. "You've been doing *what*?"

"I'm making a video that I think will save Glenna's." I hope this information will distract him from the whole approaching-potentially-hostile-strangers-on-the-street thing.

Apparently I judged right, because instead of yelling some more, he slowly says, "What do you mean?"

"Benji's art is similar to what we do at Glenna's. Helping people express themselves is really important. But hard to show on paper. So, I had this thing. I mean, there's this idea . . ." I've thought this conversation through a thousand times in my head, but for some reason, the one time it counts, I'm struggling to explain myself. I draw in a deep breath, trying to steady my nerves. "If I show my videos of Benji's art to the investment department at Knightley's, they'll see how impactful art can be. It's a long shot, I know. But it might be enough to get them to reinvest in us."

Calum's face flickers. I expect him to either agree and offer to help or yell at me for bringing up Glenna's again. Instead, he glances at his phone and says, "I've got a ton of work to do before tomorrow. We should head back."

"I—okay." I wait for him to pick up our conversation as I follow him out of the museum and towards the tube, but his face is buried in his phone, and when I peek over his shoulder, he's vigorously typing out an email.

My stomach sinks. I can't tell if he's genuinely busy or if he just doesn't want to talk about Glenna's, but I can almost see all the bonding we did this week disappearing in the space of a few tube stops. When we get home, he vanishes into his room without saying good night, shutting his door with a hard *click*.

I don't see him again until Friday.

Let's Pretend This Chapter Is About Train Station Bagels

July 1, 4:34 a.m.

Alicia: I found the Twitter you made for Glenna's.

Alicia: Why didn't you ask for my help with it?

Me: Calum's flatmate helped me set it up! She's really nice.

Alicia: I can help too if you want.

Me: That's okay, we've got it covered.

Me: But thanks for offering!!

1:18 p.m.

Alicia: Do you think you'll be around to talk soon?

Me: I'm sorry I'm really trying to find time.

Me: There's been so much going on and things aren't going well with Calum so I'm kind of stressed.

Alicia: Okay.

Alicia: But maybe soon?

2:03 p.m.

It's been four days since I brought up Glenna's to Calum, and he's completely disappeared on me. Instead of coming home from work at around five or six, he's been getting in after I'm asleep. I try to wait up for him, but my days in London have been tiring. As hard as I try, I haven't been able to keep my eyes open past eleven.

Rose tells me Calum had a work emergency and isn't avoiding me. But one night when I'm half-asleep, I hear her on the phone telling him off for taking on an extra project.

That's the last straw. Even though I'm exhausted, I force myself awake at four-freaking a.m. on Friday to catch him before he leaves for work. But when I stumble into the living room, he's already slipping out the door.

"Wait!" I yell. "When will you be home tonight?"

"Sorry," he calls, not even bothering to face me. "I'm heading to a conference in Glasgow. I won't be back until tomorrow."

"What?" I shove my foot between the door and the wall, stopping it from closing. "You're leaving London? Without me?"

Calum finally turns around, and he at least has the decency to look ashamed. "I'm sorry. My boss asked me last minute, and I can't say no. I know this isn't ideal, but Rose and Benji will be home. I'll be back before you notice I'm—"

"How will I not notice you're gone? You've been avoiding me all week!"

Calum winces. "I'm not avoiding you. I've been busy. Once this conference is over I promise I'll be around—"

"I know you've been taking on more work to avoid me because you don't want to talk about Glenna's. You keep lying. How am I supposed to ever believe anything you say?" I yank my foot back into the apartment, letting the door slam in his face.

It's less satisfying than I expect it to be.

●●●

Friday is fine. I go with Benji to collect more recordings, and on Saturday morning, he even lets me take the lead in approaching a few people. It's intimidating, asking strangers who are minding their own business for their personal stories, but I love it. It makes me feel like a part of something in a way I never really felt like a part of Glenna's. Not that I don't feel connected to Glenna's, but at home, Mom and Dad have the last word on every portrait. When I approach people with Benji, he doesn't butt in. He sometimes makes suggestions to improve my sketches, but he leaves the hearts of my drawings alive. I don't want to admit it, but it's nice being totally in charge of my art for once.

In the afternoon, Rose takes me to her mom's bookshop. I spend an hour or so walking through the aisles and comparing British words to American ones. Then I curl between the stacks and pull out my phone to check the still-unsuccessful Glenna's Twitter.

It's while I'm trying to come up with something clever to post that I get a text from my brother.

July 3, 2:35 p.m.

Calum: My train just got in. Want to meet
me at King's Cross? We can grab food if
you want.

Well, this is unexpected. I'm still annoyed, but I'm glad he's not avoiding me anymore. My heart jumps. I scowl at it.

I thought I was better at holding a grudge.

•••

Rose drops me at King's Cross and hands me off to Calum, who sits on a bench near a large train schedule. "Hi," he says when I approach.

"Hi." Now that we're face-to-face, I don't know what to do. I want to yell at him some more, but he invited me here, presumably to apologize. I bite my tongue.

Calum looks tired. He's in the immaculate work clothes he never seems to take off, and he still has his shiny briefcase. But his hair is messed up on one side like he slept against the train window, and he keeps stifling yawns with his hand. I wonder how intense his conferences are. It seems pretty unfair his boss would make him work on the weekend when he also works more than twelve hours a day during the week.

"I'm sorry I freaked out when you brought up Glenna's," he says, foregoing any attempt at small talk. "I shouldn't have avoided you this week. I was . . . I still hadn't decided if I wanted to tell you why I left home, and I knew I'd have to tell you in order to explain why I won't help with the shop. Anyway, I've decided to tell you."

It's an awful apology. I cross my arms, but I don't say anything in case it scares him off. I want to know why he left home more than I want to know anything else. Well, not *anything* else. If someone could tell me how to save Glenna's, that would be pretty nice, too.

Calum goes quiet. Opens his mouth. Closes it. "The thing is," he says finally, "I assumed you knew. It's partially why I didn't reach out earlier. But in the car, you asked why I left like it was some big mystery."

"Just say whatever you're trying to say." I pull my feet onto the bench and rest my chin on my knees.

"Yeah. Okay." He looks down at his hands, which are clenched in his lap. "You know how I ran away when I was sixteen?"

"Obviously."

"Well, that's the thing. I didn't run away."

Oh my God, I could punch him. I roll my eyes so hard, they hurt. "I guess I imagined your room has been empty for the past six years. Sorry about that. Clearly I need to get my vision checked."

Calum gives me a look that is basically its own form of eye roll. "I left home. Obviously. But I didn't run away. That makes it sound like it was my choice, but I didn't *want* to leave."

He swings his heels against the back of the bench. "I . . . when I was sixteen, I was dating someone from school. A guy from school. I wasn't ready to tell Mom and Dad, but we were a bit reckless on social media. Mom found my Instagram, and . . ." He shakes his head. "It was fine. At first. She and Dad said it didn't bother them and they still loved me and all that. But they started doing these little things. Like when Mrs. Thompson came over for dinner one night and asked if I was dating anyone, Mom said I wasn't before I could even open my mouth. Or if I was holding hands with my boyfriend in public, Mom would tell me to stop.

"I confronted her eventually, and she admitted she didn't want me to be open about being gay. She said it wasn't because she was uncomfortable—she was scared for me, and she didn't want me to be in danger. At first, I kind of appreciated the concern. But it really messed with my head to keep being told 'I love you, but you need to hide yourself. I love you, but not everyone does.' It . . . made me anxious. Paranoid. I didn't feel comfortable hanging out with my boyfriend anymore, even in private."

Calum runs his fingers through his hair, then shoves them into his pockets like he's trying to stop fidgeting. "Dad didn't police me like Mom did, but he also never stopped her. Every time I explained how much it was affecting me, they said I was being dramatic. I couldn't live like that. I couldn't keep screaming into empty space. So I . . . left."

He trails off. I frown, trying to process what he said. Calum left home because . . . Mom cared a lot about him? Like, okay. I'm sure it was frustrating when he told Mom she was being overprotective and she didn't listen, but she doesn't listen to anyone. I'm literally in another country right now because Mom didn't listen to me! Heat flares in my stomach. *This* is the reason I didn't grow up with my brother? "They were right," I snap. "You *were* being dramatic. What parents don't try to control their kids? It's a normal thing. It's not a reason to run away!"

Calum's eyes flash. "Maisie, I'm ten years older than you. Crescent Valley might be different now, but I didn't grow up with people telling me it was okay to be gay. I never even heard the word until I was eleven and someone yelled it at me during recess. My friends used it as an insult. Adults used it to make fun of people they didn't want to be associated with. When I realized I maybe *was* that word—" He breaks off and glares at his hands, which are clenched in his lap. After a moment, he continues.

"When I was in middle school and teachers asked where we pictured ourselves in twenty years, I . . . couldn't. It felt like there wasn't any space in the world for me, like I wasn't allowed to exist. So when Mom and Dad's reaction to finding out I was gay was to act like the only future I had was one where I needed to hide—" Calum breaks off. "It wasn't some little thing, Maisie. It was my *life*."

Oh. A few years ago, when Alicia told me she had a crush on Erica, she said it in the same tone of voice she might use to announce the weather. Neither of us blinked. It wasn't a big deal, and yeah, a few chaperones looked twice when she and Erica went to the fifth-grade dance together. But even then, the glances weren't mean—they were just curious.

I grew up that way, with people barely blinking. No one in Crescent Valley thinks twice about what you wear or who you date or what your hobbies are, so it's hard to imagine my town not always being like it is now.

But it's even harder to wrap my head around the other stuff. The inside stuff Calum mentioned about not being able to picture his future. Whenever I feel like I don't fit in, Mom and Dad tell me

I'm perfect and should just be myself. But what if I hadn't grown up being told that? What if the people around me had said *You don't fit in? Well, that's your own fault.*

I look down at my knees, which are jumping up and down on the bench. "I'm sorry," I mutter. "I didn't mean to make you upset. This is just a lot of information and it kind of came out of nowhere."

Calum's voice softens. "I know. And it seems like Mom and Dad are doing a better job at raising you than they did with me, so I don't want this to affect your relationship with them. That's why I didn't tell you sooner, and I'm only telling you now because I need you to understand why I can't help with Glenna's. I can't be involved in something where I might have to interact with them. They . . . it's not like they never apologized. They know they messed up. But I'm still angry."

He clears his throat. "Anyway. The real reason I brought you to King's Cross is for the food. There are a lot of options here, but . . . on second thought, I'm not sure why you'd want to eat in a train station. We can just go to a restaurant. Or . . . there is a place in here that sells bagels. It's so hard to find bagels in London."

I don't answer right away. Calum is pale, and his hands are pressed hard against the bench. He looks super uncomfortable, which is probably why he's changing the subject. I don't want to keep talking about something that makes him uncomfortable, but there's one more thing I have to ask.

I tread carefully. "You know now, right? That you're allowed to exist?"

Calum freezes. It takes a second for me to work up the nerve to look at him. When I do, he nods.

"Okay. Good." I jump to my feet, trying to shake off my emotions. There are a lot of them—too many—and I don't want Calum to see them crawling over my skin. I try for a smile. It definitely looks forced. "I could go for a bagel. Even a train station bagel."

He stands. I follow him through the station, and a minute later we're arguing over which deli has the best bagels in New York.

Alicia Betrays Me

When we get home from King's Cross, I call Aunt Lisa. I need more information about this Calum situation, and I need it now.

"Maisie?" Aunt Lisa picks up on the third ring. "This is a surprise. Is everything all right?"

"It's fine. London's good. I'm good. But—um." Do I jump right into this? I'm not usually the person who brings up serious things. Whenever something intense happens, it's always Mom sitting me down on the sapphire couch. "Um." I try again, treading lightly. "I was wondering if you could tell me something?"

"A specific something? Or would you like a random fact? I've got one of those apps on my phone that tells me a new word every day. It's quite fun. I've learned many a—"

"Calum told me he didn't run away from home. Well, he kind of ran away. But he told me why."

"Oh." I hear a *thump* as Aunt Lisa sits down. I expect her to keep talking, but she doesn't.

"He . . ." I hesitate, trying to turn the emotions in my head into words. "He explained why he left, and I get it. Kind of. But also, not really? Mom wanted him to hide his relationship, which obviously wouldn't feel good. But to leave home? For *six years*?

Isn't that . . . a little dramatic?" Calum got angry when I asked him that at King's Cross, but it feels like a valid question. I mean, he's held this grudge for half my life?!

Aunt Lisa sighs. "When Calum first arrived at my flat, he wouldn't tell me the details of what happened with your mum and dad, but I could see how he felt, and that was enough."

I think back to King's Cross. In the time I've known Calum, his emotions have always been under the surface. I can usually tell when he's happy or frustrated, but sometimes I really have to squint. When he was telling me about home, though, I didn't even have to look at him to know how he was feeling. His emotions were crawling over his skin—I could feel them in his voice and his movements, in the nervous energy crackling between his shoulder and mine on the bench.

"Sometimes people go through things we can't understand," Aunt Lisa continues. "But that doesn't mean what happened is any less real. Pain doesn't have to be bloody to hurt."

I think I get what she means. When you can see an injury, it's obvious why it hurts. But when there's no blood, it's easy to think the person who's complaining is being dramatic. At King's Cross, Calum was upset. I couldn't totally see why, but I could see that he was. Maybe that's all that matters. "I shouldn't have said he overreacted," I mutter.

"No," Aunt Lisa agrees, "but you know better now, and that's the important bit."

My vision goes blurry. It takes me a second to realize why. Mom and Dad aren't the same people they were when Calum was a teenager. If I ever have a crush on someone who isn't a boy, I know they'll never make me hide my relationship. They've told me as much since before I even knew what dating was, and I know this applies to other things, too. If one day I decide I hate Glenna's and want to be a pastry chef or something, it won't be a problem. Mom and Dad are controlling in a lot of ways, but not over the things that matter.

Except they told me Calum ran away. They made it seem like it was *his* decision to leave. If they've learned from their mistakes, why did they lie to me?

The world drips like wet paint, heavy and blurring at the edges. Everything I thought I knew about my family is peeling away, and I can't see what's left behind. "They lied. My parents lied to me." I hate how shaky my voice sounds.

"Oh, hon. You were so young when this happened. My guess is they thought they were protecting you—"

"From who? Themselves?" I close my eyes. If I'd known Calum didn't leave home because he hated us—because he hated *me*—I would have looked for him. I would have found him, and I could have grown up knowing him—even if we lived on opposite sides of an ocean. But because my parents were too scared to tell me the truth, my brother is a stranger to me. Well, not as much anymore, but he was for six years.

For half my life.

"I have to go," I mutter into the phone. "Thanks for talking to me."

I hang up before Aunt Lisa can respond. I expect tears to fall immediately—they've been building behind my eyes since before I opened my phone, and the pressure is becoming more and more painful. I want to explode, to feel that release. But for some reason, my eyes remain dry.

I reach for my phone. There's only one person who might be able to make me feel better.

I press her number.

She doesn't answer.

July 3, 6:34 p.m.

> Me: Something intense happened. Can you pick up??

No answer. I check the clock. It's late in Crescent Valley, but not late enough for Alicia to be asleep. My throat clenches. Did something happen? I can't handle another disaster right now.

●●●

I don't hear from Alicia for three hours. Finally, my phone dings.

9:36 p.m.

Alicia: Camping with Rowan and my parents in the Adirondacks for the weekend.
Alicia: You can try texting but service is awful.
Alicia: I'll call when I'm home.

Great.

I Do Something Bad

I blame Alicia for what I do next. Okay, not really. But if she'd picked up the phone, I probably wouldn't have called Mom and Dad. Without her to talk me down . . .

The TV in the living room is blasting with some show that Calum, Benji, and Rose watch every week. While they're distracted, I call my parents.

And I explode.

"Maisie!" Mom says when she picks up. "Nice of you to call us first for once."

I can't believe she sounds so *happy*. Rage crashes like a tide against my rib cage, ebbing and flowing, ebbing and flowing.

"Hello?" Mom says when I don't respond. "You're on speaker. Dad and I are in the workshop—"

"I KNOW WHAT YOU DID TO CALUM WHAT'S WRONG-WITH YOU?"

The line goes quiet. I'm not sure if they're trying to decipher my screaming, or if they understood and I shocked them into silence.

After what feels like six years, Mom says, very quietly, "Maisie."

She understood, then.

My fingers are clenched into claws and my arms are shaking from the force of it and I want to scream again but I don't know what to say. There's nothing I can say that will express how angry I am, and this realization somehow makes me even angrier.

"What's wrong with you?" It's not a scream. It's barely a breath. I close my eyes and lean back against my pillow. "Why didn't you listen to him? Why didn't you *tell me why he left?*"

"Maisie—" It's Dad this time, but I don't let him finish. Whatever he says will just be an excuse.

"I'm not coming home. Ever. I'm staying with Calum. Don't call me again." I hang up, turn my phone to airplane mode, and bury my head in my pillow before my brain can catch up with my mouth. I try to sleep.

I don't.

●●●

The sun rises through the gaps in the blinds. I watch it dully, tracking the shadows on the floor as they shorten and stretch. My eyes are dry, but in an itchy way, like they need to be watered.

I rotate my itchy eyes toward Rose. She's still asleep—I was awake when she came into the room last night, and I was awake when she fell asleep, and I'm still awake waiting for her alarm to ring in three hours' time. I'm so tired that I'm not anymore. My brain buzzes like it does when I sneakily drink coffee behind my parents' back.

I roll onto my side and grab my phone. I hesitate, then take it off airplane mode. Not because I want to talk to my parents but because I haven't forgotten that Mom said if I ever cut contact with her again, the consequences would be severe.

Unlike when I ran away from Aunt Lisa's, I don't have any missed calls. I only have four texts. From Dad.

July 3, 18:15 p.m.

Dad: Maisie, you can't turn your phone off.
Dad: You can be angry, but we need to be able to reach you.
Dad: This is serious.
Dad: Call us back.

There's something about seeing his name that makes me want to scream. The thing is, Mom is stubborn. Once she got in her head that she thought she knew what was best for Calum, it tracks with her personality that she wouldn't have changed her mind. But Dad is different. He always stands up for me when it matters, and this mattered more than anything. How could he not have taken Calum's side? It makes no sense.

I stare at his messages. When I said I was never coming home last night, I didn't mean it. Not in the way Calum meant it. But there's nothing my parents can do that will make things okay. They hurt Calum. They lied to me.

I hesitate. Maybe there is one thing.

July 4, 6:00 a.m.

Me: Apologize to Calum. If you do that, I'll call you back.

Calum said Mom and Dad have apologized over the years, but I don't know how sincere those apologies were. If they want to prove they've learned from their mistakes, they should reach out properly and take responsibility for what they did.

6:01 a.m.

Dad: We don't have his number.

I give it to him. Then I turn my phone back to airplane mode and stare at the ceiling until Rose's alarm wakes her a few hours later.

Calum and Benji are already in the living room when we head to breakfast. They wave, oblivious to the itchy feeling behind my eyes. I nod but don't say anything. I'm staring at Calum's phone, which sits next to a box of cereal on the table. I wonder if Mom and Dad already called him. I'm about to ask, when his screen suddenly lights up with Mom's number.

Coffee spills from Calum's mug as it clatters to the table. He blinks hard, like he's trying to clear his eyes to make sure he's seeing right. The call ends, but a few seconds later, his phone buzzes again.

He stares at it like it's a bomb. "Did someone die?"

I try to hide my smile, but I may have just single-handedly glued our family back together. "It's nothing bad," I say through my grin. "I promise."

Calum slowly peels his eyes off the phone and looks at me. Maybe I should have given more thought to how he'd react to Mom calling, because he doesn't seem pleasantly surprised or excited like I expected. When I look at his face, all I see is . . . rage.

He jerks his chin at the phone. "Did you give her my number?"

My insides squeeze. I've had my fair share of fights with my brother since coming to London, but this is the first time I hear real, dark anger in his voice. It's confusing, and it makes me want to lie. But he already knows the truth from when I smiled.

"After what you told me yesterday, I was so angry." My voice is too loud in this silent room. "I yelled at Mom and Dad. They asked me to let them explain, but I said I wouldn't unless they apologized to you."

Calum stares at me for another long moment. Then he flings his phone off the table. It smacks the floor and bounces out of sight. I nearly jump out of my skin.

"Damn it, Maisie." He stands so violently that his chair clatters to the ground. "What is *wrong* with you?"

The words cut into me, leaving me speechless. I can't break eye contact with him, even though I feel the heat of his glower like a burn on my cheeks. We're both frozen for what feels like an eternity. Finally, Calum kicks his chair back and spins around. He leaves the kitchen and a door slams. We're left with silence except for the dull buzzing of his phone from somewhere behind the couch.

I look at Rose and Benji. Rose is a statue, a spoonful of cereal halfway to her mouth. Benji hesitates, then crouches to search for Calum's phone. When he finds it, he places it gingerly on the table. There's a crack in the screen, but it's not broken, and it's still buzzing with calls from Mom.

"I—I didn't mean—" I cut off. My voice still sounds too loud.

Benji and Rose glance at each other. I can't tell if they're also mad at me. After a pause, Benji claps a hand on my shoulder. It doesn't feel like an angry clap, but when he speaks, his words aren't for me. "Can you take her out of the flat? She needs to leave for a while."

She needs to leave for a while. I hear that over and over and over until there's no room in my head for anything else.

Rose nods at Benji. Then she turns and gives me a small smile. It doesn't quite reach her eyes. "Let's get dressed, yeah? We'll go somewhere nice."

I'm too frozen to respond.

●●●

Rose takes me to Hyde Park. It's bright and beautiful, and on another day, I'd be itching for my sketchpad. Right now, though, my whole body feels tight. I'm not sure if it's tears or hurt or confusion or what, but there are a lot of things fighting for space inside me. I barely pay attention to our surroundings until we stop by a lake full of swans.

I've never seen a swan in real life, and it's enough to distract me for a second. They're larger than I imagined, and way more majestic. Snow white and haughty and with every feather in place. A few kids chase them by the bank, but when I take a step forward, Rose says, "I wouldn't get too close, as they're actually quite aggressive. But did you know the queen owns them?"

"Really?" I look back at the swans. They don't have markings or tags on them like I sometimes see at the zoo. "How does she know which are hers?"

"They're all hers," Rose says. "She owns all the swans in England."

I roll my eyes, but she raises her hands in defense. "It's true! Google it."

I can't. I'm not connected to Wi-Fi. But speaking of phones . . .

I look down. "Why is he so mad at me?" I don't need to elaborate.

Rose jerks her head toward a bench. I follow her over to it, and we sit. I stare at the swans as the wind blows hair into my eyes. After a few moments, Rose says, "Do you know what an ally is?"

I swing my legs back and forth through the air, as if I'm on a swing. "It's when people team up to do something together. Like in a war or a trivia night or something."

"Yes," Rose says, smiling slightly, "but it can also be used to describe someone who wants to stand up for people who have struggles that are different from their own. I'll give you an example. When I'm looking for people to date, I only want to date guys. It's expected that girls want to date guys, so I've never had anyone hurt me or say mean things when I have a boyfriend. But there are people like Calum who do get hurt or have mean things said to them because of who they date. I want to help those people to have less struggles, but I'm not actually one of them. That means I do my best to be an ally. Do you understand?"

I stop swinging my legs and cross my ankles. "Yeah, but I'm not sure why you're telling me this."

Rose shifts her body so she's facing me on the bench. I finally turn away from the swans to look at her. "Calum had to leave home because he's gay. You're angry and upset at your parents, which is so understandable. But you aren't the one who had to leave."

"Which means I'd be an ally. I get that, but I still don't—"

Rose reaches out and gently squeezes my hand. I close my mouth. "The thing that's tricky about being an ally is you don't actually get to decide if you are one. Even if you think you're helping someone, it's easy to overstep. You can be angry at your parents. Of course you can. But it's not your place to tell them to reach out to Calum. You aren't the person they hurt."

"But they *did* hurt me." I don't want to get riled up, but clearly neither she nor Calum understands this is also hard for me.

I try to explain. "Our parents are the reason Calum had to leave. *Our* parents. They aren't just his. They lied to me. They disappointed me. They made me scared to trust them. I'm still involved, even though—"

Rose nods. "I can't imagine how horrible and overwhelming this must all feel. It makes perfect sense that you're upset, and you have every right to be. But . . ." She lowers her voice, maybe to soften the blow of her words. "It's because you're upset that you reached out to your parents, right? The reason you want them to apologize to Calum is because it will make you feel better?"

I wipe at my eyes. There still aren't any tears, and I'm furious that I've apparently lost the ability to cry. "Why are you saying that like it's a bad thing? Yeah, their apology would make me feel better, but it would also make Calum feel better. His life will be so much easier once he forgives them."

Rose squeezes my hand again. "But why should you get to decide if Calum forgives them? You didn't even know about all this until yesterday. He's been dealing with it for six years."

My cheeks flood with heat, because . . . oh. If I'd stopped to consider Calum's feelings for even one second, I probably would have realized how terrible my idea was. My parents needed me to give them Calum's phone number so they could apologize. I didn't think anything of that in the moment, but it obviously means Calum never gave it to them himself.

There's a prickly feeling running up my arms. I think it's embarrassment. Or maybe shame. I look down. "I thought I was doing a good thing."

Rose nods. "I know, and Calum knows, too. But that's why being an ally is so difficult. Even when you have the best intentions, you've got to stop and think about whether you're actually being supportive."

I haven't been able to meet Rose's eyes for a while. She nudges my arm until I do. Her face is open. Kind. Even though I did something so wrong. Bile rises in my throat.

"This is complicated," Rose continues. "It takes time to learn. Your heart was in the right place, which is a great start. But next time, remember your brain is important, too."

My eyes itch again. I didn't mean to make this about me. Then again, I didn't exactly try not to. "I'm sorry," I mutter, even though Rose isn't the person I should be saying that to.

She pulls me in for a hug. Like this, with her freckled arms holding me, with her curly hair in my face, I've never been reminded more of Alicia. I miss her so much. I miss home before this summer, before I knew everything I do now.

We stay like this for a moment. Finally, when I feel a little better, I pull away. Rose is looking into the distance. I follow her gaze back to the gleeful children and the swans. "One last thing," she says. "Calum rarely talks about home. The few times he's mentioned his parents to me, it wasn't because he wanted me to yell at them, and it wasn't even because he wanted me to comfort him. He just wanted someone to listen." She smiles softly. "Listening is underrated. It's usually the most helpful thing we can do."

I pick at the end of my ponytail. "But what if he doesn't want me to listen anymore? What if I . . ." I lower my voice to a whisper. "What if I ruined everything?"

Rose hesitates. Then she leans forward like she has a secret. "If I tell you something, do you promise to keep it between us?"

I nod.

She continues in a hushed voice. "When Calum found you in Edinburgh, he said he was in Scotland for work, right? The truth is, that was a cover."

My eyes widen. "So he really is a spy?"

Rose freezes. Then she bursts out laughing. "That isn't where I was going with this, but listen. He absolutely is. At a party last year, when we were drinking—er, apple juice—"

I glower at her. "I know what alcohol is."

Rose nods in surrender. "I suppose I can't have a complicated conversation about allyship with you and then pretend you're too young to know about alcohol. Anyway, we were at a party last year drinking—not apple juice—and I was suddenly inspired to write an essay outlining precisely why I'm convinced Calum works for MI6. It's twenty pages, single-spaced, and my best work to date. I can send it to you if you'd like. *However*, we have strayed from my point."

She leans an arm against the back of the bench. "Calum wasn't in Edinburgh for work. The moment he heard you were in Scotland, he took the day off and drove to find you. Benji and I didn't even know he'd left London until he texted from the hotel."

My eyebrows rise skeptically. "But you and Benji were so surprised when he brought me to your apartment. You thought he'd kidnapped me."

Rose waves a hand. "Calum is very fun to tease, and we take every opportunity." Her face grows more serious. "He really did drive to Edinburgh just for you."

Oh.

I try to smile, but if anything, now I feel worse. Calum wanted to meet me so badly that he took off work and drove seven hours to another country without knowing if I'd even agree to come to London? Meanwhile, I didn't care enough to spend a single second considering how he'd feel if I gave his number to our parents.

My expression must drop, because Rose says, "It might not seem like it, because Calum was taught by Britain's top agents to never express any emotions, but he cares about you very much. I highly doubt you ruined everything."

She might be right. But the thing is . . .

I pretended to come to London to get to know my brother, when really I just wanted to save Glenna's. I lied to him, even though I knew he genuinely wanted to spend time with me. And then he trusted me with something personal, and I was careless with it.

I was careless, even though I'm not just here for Glenna's anymore.

"I've been so selfish." I barely whisper the words. I don't think Rose hears, but that's okay. I said them for me.

●●●

Rose tells me to give Calum some more time, so we hang in Hyde Park a bit longer, grab lunch, and spend the rest of the day at the British Museum. After dinner, we finally return to the flat and—after nearly an hour of trying to work up the courage—I knock on my brother's door. "It's me," I say, way more shakily than I practiced.

There's a pause. "Come in."

I take a breath, then slip inside the room. It takes me a second to find Calum in the mess. Paper litters his floor, his desk—even his bed. Most of the stacks are white with official-looking black text, but a few scraps of color hide below the work assignments. I see some of Benji in here, as well. His sketchbook is splayed across the desk, his sunflower jacket is flung over the chair, and a pair of his boots peeks out from under the bed. There are three bedrooms in the flat, so I assumed one of them was Benji's. Are there three bedrooms? There are three doors, but I never checked behind the last one. Maybe it's actually a closet or shower. It only now occurs to me this might be why Calum made me sleep on Rose's floor instead of his own.

My brother stands next to his wardrobe. When I see what he's wearing, I'm kind of taken aback. He's in normal clothes—flannel pajamas and a baggy black shirt—but that's what's so shocking. This is the first time I've seen him not in a suit. Without it, he looks a lot less put together.

He watches me warily.

I pull at my hair. It falls over one shoulder, and I can't seem to look up from it. "I'm sorry," I mumble from behind the curtain of blond.

Calum sits on his bed. He doesn't look murderous like he did this morning. He just looks tired.

"Maisie, I know this isn't fair. You shouldn't be caught in the middle of my stuff with Mom and Dad. But telling them to reach out to me? That's also not fair." He turns sideways, so I can only see his profile. "I like my life in London. I'm happy now, but I—" He cuts off, twisting his hands in his blankets. "If I could have stayed in Crescent Valley, if I could have a relationship with Mom and Dad without . . ." He shakes his head. Starts over. "Maisie, I don't like being separated from our family. Don't you understand? None of this has been *easy*."

"I'm sorry," I say quietly, and I feel ridiculous, because all those tears that wouldn't fall over the past day are suddenly streaming down my cheeks. I don't want to cry in front of him, but now that I am, I can't seem to stop. "I'm sorry for calling you dramatic at King's Cross. I'm sorry for telling Mom and Dad to reach out to you. I—" I swipe at my eyes. "If you . . . I can go back to Aunt Lisa's, if you want. Or if she won't take me, I can go home—"

Calum's brows furrow. "You want to leave?"

I wipe snot from my face with my sleeve. "Don't . . . you want me to?"

I'm not looking at him, so I don't realize he's gotten up from the bed until his arms are tentatively wrapping around me. I go rigid, because this is weird. But the longer he holds me, the less weird it feels, so after a few moments, I hug him back.

"I don't want you to leave," he says as I cry into his shirt. "Please don't leave. But don't try to Parent Trap me again. You kind of tried to Parent Trap me."

"What's Parent Trap?"

Calum lets out a fake gasp, but it loses its drama because it sounds kind of watery. "Am I really that much older than you?"

"Eighty-five is pretty old."

"Ouch." He shakes slightly. It takes me a second to realize he's not crying. He's laughing.

"I'm sorry," I say into his shoulder. "I mean, not for calling you eighty-five. You are eighty-five. But I shouldn't have asked Mom and Dad to reach out to you. That was selfish."

Calum pulls away, but keeps hold of my shoulders. "It's okay. But . . ."

I wipe at my nose. "What?"

He lets his hands fall. "You weren't trying to hurt me. I know that, but it . . . doesn't change the fact that you did. I'm not saying that to upset you; I just need you to understand—" He shakes his head.

"You called me dramatic at King's Cross. So many people use that word when they find out why I left home, but dramatic— why is it a bad thing? Being dramatic is just another way of saying someone is taking up space, and I'm allowed to do that. I am allowed to exist, but Mom and Dad made it so I couldn't take up space in *my own home*. I don't need you—or want you—to understand how that feels. But you do need to know it's not something that just goes away. This—it changed how I see the world, how I interact with it. So maybe Mom and Dad have learned to do better, but that doesn't magically mean I didn't go through what I did."

Calum draws in a breath. "Like I said, this isn't an attack. But it is an explanation for why I've . . . I've decided I can't talk about Mom or Dad or home with you anymore. Not because I want to punish you, or because I don't think you'll learn, or—"

"I get it." I do. I hurt him in a tender place, like kicking someone's already broken leg, and he's protecting the wound. On top of that, Rose said he rarely talks about home anyway, so it's probably not been easy to have all these discussions with me over the past few days. It's not personal. I know it's not, but it still feels like he's slammed a door closed that I'd finally managed to crack open. The *thump* reverberates in my chest; once the dust settles, I'm left looking at less of my brother than was in front of me before.

Calum runs a hand through his hair and tries to make eye contact with me, but we both look away. "I'm sure you still have questions about—" He waves a hand in the general direction of everything. "I don't mind if you talk to Mom or Dad or anyone else about what happened. You can ask anything, I just can't be the one to give you answers. I'm sorry."

I shake my head. "I should be saying that."

"You already did." Calum hesitates. Then he holds out a hand. "Are we good?"

I scrunch my nose at him. "You hugged me a second ago."

"That was a one-time thing."

"We're not coworkers in your stuffy office."

"My office is not stuffy."

"I've been here for weeks and this is the first time I've seen you not in a suit."

Calum frowns. "There is nothing wrong with suits."

"I didn't say there was anything *wrong* with them. Just that they're—"

He jerks his head at the door. "You can go now." He says it sharply, but he's not angry. I can tell now, when he's faking.

I try to top his fake anger by huffing loudly as I walk out. But in the hallway, I pause, looking at the thin slab of door between us. Two weeks ago, I admitted it hurt when Calum left home, but I don't think I realized the reason it hurt is because I missed him. Not the person he was—we weren't close when he lived in Crescent Valley. But I missed the idea of him, the person he might have become after he left, the person I would never know.

Now I'll never know everything. He said I can ask other people about what happened at home, but it's not the same as hearing it in his own words.

I blink hard. My emotions are being selfish again. I know that, but I can't just turn them off when they're ugly.

I can't turn them off, but . . . Rose said when it comes to Calum, I have to use my brain as well as my heart. My heart is already feeling out plans to convince him to open back up to me. But my brain . . . when I think about the past two days, I see Calum at King's Cross after he finally told me why he left home, picking at his bagel with his fingers but never taking a bite. I see him on the tube, tearing at his nails once the bagel was in shreds, barely responding to my babbling attempts to fill the silence. And I see him at the table this morning, his face deathly white when Mom's number popped up on his phone.

As hard as it is for me not to ask Calum about home, it is clearly so much harder for him to talk about it. So I won't ask. I won't come up with plans to try and change his mind. Not about this. Not ever.

But inside my own head, where they can't harm anyone else, I let my emotions be selfish. For the rest of the night, I think about how Calum shut me out. It hurts.

I let it.

I Have Feelings and They Hurt

You know how people say the best way to feel better about something is to talk about it? Yeah. I don't do that.

Calum said I could ask Mom and Dad anything I want about what happened when he lived at home. I do have questions, but . . . I'm still so angry. My parents didn't listen to Calum. They lied to me. Right now, I don't want anything to do with them.

I don't want anything to do with them, but my whole body starts pulsing with guilt every time their names pop up on my phone. After I ran away to London, Mom said the consequences would be severe if I ever cut contact with her again. And the thing is, Mom is good at punishments. Losing my phone or TV privileges? That's too easy. Instead, she usually takes away Glenna's. Sometimes that means hiding my graphite pencils or locking me out of the workshop for a week, but the worst was the time I snuck over to Alicia's house for a sleepover after Mom said I couldn't go. She and Dad thought I'd died in a ditch or something because they couldn't find me all night, and yeah, I shouldn't have scared them. But as punishment, Mom took away a sketch for a portrait I'd spent more than three days designing. The sound of my paper being torn from the easel still sets my teeth on edge, but the worst part is, she never gave it back.

If Mom stole my sketch because I scared her for a few hours, what will she do now that I'm in a totally different country and refusing to answer my phone? For all my parents know, I really *could* be dead in a ditch. When they finally get ahold of me (and they will, because they're Mom and Dad), will they ban me from Glenna's forever? Will they find The Book in my room and burn it? I shiver.

I shiver, but I don't break. I'm allowed to be upset. I won't let my parents take that away from me, not even if it means my brain will imagine a billion horrific punishments for the next few weeks.

Speaking of anger, I'm also mad at Alicia. I understand not having cell service while she was in the mountains, but it's been days since she saw my desperate texts the night Calum told me what happened at home. There's no way she's still camping in the Adirondacks, which means she's ignoring me. I need her so badly, and she doesn't care.

She doesn't care.

I grab my phone and start to type.

July 9, 11:07 p.m.

Me: You promised at the beginning of the summer that you still wanted to be friends.

Me: I needed you this weekend.

Me: You weren't there.

She doesn't respond.

We Don't Go to Jail for Feeding Swans

The next week, I don't have time to save Glenna's or go to class. Lying on my floor bed without changing clothes and staring at the ceiling until my eyes blur is a twenty-four-hour-a-day job.

Calum, Rose, and Benji seem to realize this, because they leave me alone. Except for at meals, where someone always forces me to get up and come to the table. I don't fight them, because (1) I'm hungry, and (2) they let me glare at my plate in silence, so it's almost like I'm still alone with my ceiling.

On Saturday, though, Calum pulls me up from my blankets and marches me out of the flat. "Enough wallowing," he says when I protest.

We step outside, and I'm momentarily blinded. I've spent so much time hiding from the sun like a vampire that I almost burst into flames right on the doorstep. After a minute, though, the warmth feels pretty nice. The wind feels nice. Even the exhaust from the buses and cars is kind of nice, because it smells like something other than my floor bed.

Calum watches me carefully, as though calculating the odds of whether I'm about to have a breakdown on the pavement. He looks a little like he did when he handed me that Barbie in the car: hopeful but unsure.

I smile. Even though I miss my ceiling, I do feel better now that I'm no longer staring at it. Calum, seemingly satisfied that dragging me out of the house was not a horrible mistake, nods once and starts walking. I run to catch up.

It's been a while since we've done anything together. Not because things have been awkward—I thought they might be, but since our fight, Calum has tried to take me to high tea, the Tate Modern, and some bakery he likes. I turned him down every time in favor of lying on the floor, but now that I remember how nice the outside world is, I kind of wish I'd at least said yes to the museum.

I don't know where he's taking me today. Every time I ask, he just says, "Nearly there," and keeps walking. Eventually, we reach a park. Kensington Gardens, Calum says it's called. I assume we're going to ride bikes or a boat or something, but instead he leads me over to a bench and sits. I hesitate. "Did you bring me here to feed the swans?"

"God no. Give them one piece of bread and they'll chase you all the way home."

"That sounds fun."

"We have different definitions of 'fun.'"

"Uhhhh . . . *clearly*. The finance museum? I'm still in physical pain from that." I sit down next to him. "Why are we here?" I ask again.

Calum opens his briefcase and pulls out two sketchpads, as well as a small collection of fancy colored pencils. I stare at him, uncomprehending.

He hesitates. "You haven't done art—or anything, really—in days. So I thought . . . we could draw. If you want."

He pushes one of the sketchpads at me, but I don't take it. I can't, when I'm so busy gaping at him. "You want to . . . draw. With me?"

"If you want." Calum sets the sketchpad next to me on the bench and opens the other one, flipping to a blank page. "I lied, earlier. When I said I didn't like it."

"I know." I slowly take the pad and place it in my lap. "Benji told me you have a web comic and that you sometimes do street art with him."

Calum's lip twitches. "Is there anything Benji hasn't told you?"

I look down. "He didn't tell me why you lied."

Calum picks up a green pencil and presses it to his pad. "I thought if I told you about my art, you would have pestered me nonstop about saving Glenna's."

I don't have a retort for that, because—yeah. I totally would have.

I pull a pink pencil from the case, drawing flowers in one corner of my page. "When did you start liking art? You never spent time in the workshop when we were li—sorry," I amend quickly. "I won't bring up—"

Calum shakes his head. "I don't mind talking about this." He reaches for a blue pencil. "Before you were born—ouch, am I really that much older than you?"

"We've established that you're a hundred and two."

"I thought I was eighty-five."

"You've aged since then."

Calum glances at me. "I don't remember getting any birthday presents."

"You can have my drawing when it's finished."

"I'd prefer a cake."

"Buy yourself a cake."

"Anyway," he continues, "Before you were born, I loved Glenna's. Truly. I used to spend hours in the workshop—painting, drawing, sometimes just lying on the ground with a book. It was my favorite place. But . . ." He reaches for a yellow pencil. I grab a black one. "Don't take this the wrong way, but when you were born and started getting into art, I suppose I got a bit jealous."

My pencil pauses. I glance over at him. "Jealous? Of what?"

Calum gives me a look like the answer is super obvious, but I really have no idea what he's talking about. "By the time you were six, your figure drawings were more accurate than mine. You've got a very traditional style, while I've always been more abstract. And Glenna's is all about realistic art, so your work was more in line with the business. Mom and Dad used to hang my paintings alongside yours, but I never felt like mine fit with the rest of the house. So I . . . never stopped drawing, but I began to do it in private, just for myself." He grimaces. "I'm aware there's an ironic metaphor for my life in there. We're ignoring it."

Now that I really think about it, I do remember Calum drawing when we were younger. He worked on his own instead of with Dad and me, but I would sometimes walk past his room and see him sitting on his floor, covered in pencils. I don't remember ever getting a good look at his art aside from the sunset painting in the living room, but if his style is always as abstract as that piece, he's right that it wouldn't match with the rest of the house. I don't think that's a bad thing, but I can see how it would be frustrating.

"I'm sorry."

He shrugs. "It's not your fault. It wasn't even Mom and Dad's fault. It's just . . . how it was. Anyway, I'm at least glad it gave me the push to start my web comic. There's nothing quite like doing art for yourself, is there?"

"I wouldn't know," I answer truthfully.

Calum's eyebrows draw together. "I follow your Instagram. You post sketches all the time."

"Those are for Glenna's. I paint landscapes sometimes, but mainly as practice for portrait backgrounds. And Alicia and I are working on an art poetry book, but . . ." I trail off. At the start of the summer, when Mom said I needed to find passions outside of Glenna's, I thought she was being ridiculous. When Aunt Lisa told me she left Glenna's because she wanted to make something of her own, I didn't think she understood the importance of our shop. But now I'm having this conversation with *another* person? I scratch at the side of my pencil with my nail. "Is it bad if I don't do art just for myself?"

Calum shrugs. "Not necessarily. Benji's art is for other people. Anyone who runs a shop makes art for consumers. Even my web comic—I initially created it for me, but now I post it publicly. That influences the way I tell the story." He glances at me. "As long as you're satisfied with what you're making, it doesn't matter who it's for. You love working for Glenna's. I get that, but . . . why do you love it? Specifically?"

A few weeks ago, I thought I'd figured that out. Aside from the legacy aspect of the shop, I love Glenna's because of its message: We use our art to help people express themselves. But do we really deserve to run a store with that message after what my parents did to Calum?

I pick up a purple pencil, but I don't press it to the page. Glenna's isn't mine. It's my family's, and I love it for that. But I'm also furious at my family right now, which means there's no way to separate the thing I love most from the people I'm angriest at.

I feel the same way about The Book. I love that it's more than just mine, but every time I've thought about it this summer, I've been reminded of how far apart Alicia and I have grown. We've barely talked since I've been abroad—one video call, a few texts here and there. And now, with her not responding to my angry messages from early in the week, thinking about The Book just makes me sad.

I think I get it now, why people make things that are just for themselves.

I run my finger over the edge of my sketchpad. "I love art because of Glenna's," I say finally. "I would be a totally different person if I didn't love art, and I don't know if I would like that other person."

Calum nods. "I love art because of Glenna's, too."

I shade the bottom of my page green. My drawing is coming together nicely, but . . . if I didn't know better, I'd think it was done by Dad. His style is my style. His color choices are my color choices. There is absolutely nothing about this piece that screams *Maisie made that!* It's not unique to me in any way.

My lip trembles. I press my teeth into it. "How do you . . ." I have to take a breath before finishing my question. "How do you learn to make something that's yours? That looks like you, I mean. That doesn't look like anyone else."

Calum seems to consider for a moment. "You just have to draw, I think? Some of it will be terrible, and some of it will be great, and eventually you'll see yourself in the mess." He sets down his pencil and turns his sketchpad for me to see. Based on his words, I have no idea what I'll find on his page. I lean closer, and . . .

Oh.

He drew the same thing as me.

It's us. Sitting on this bench in the park. I show him my picture so we can compare. He was right: My art is much more traditional than his—very Glenna's, with realistic proportions and lots of details. Calum's style is more sketch-like. In his version, we're shadows instead of solid people, and the sky, grass, water, and flowers all merge together at the edges. It's not sloppy, though. Every stroke looks intentional, and his shading is flawless.

"Your lines are so dynamic," I say.

Calum scoffs. "You're a much better artist than me. Objectively."

"Don't be ridiculous. Look at your blending! I could never get colors like that."

"If you like it so much . . ." He rips his drawing out of the sketchpad and hands it to me. "Happy Birthday."

I tear mine out as well. "You're the one turning a hundred and three."

"I thought I was a hundred and two."

"You were, but now it's your birthday. Don't you know how birthdays work?"

He shakes his head. "I must be too old to remember."

"That's okay. I'm here to remind you."

"I know." Calum throws my drawing back at me, but it catches the wind and smacks him in the face.

I cackle.

Sometimes People Aren't Awful

On Sunday morning, I open my text chain with my parents. I'm not ready to have a full-blown conversation with them, but I am kind of worried they'll send Aunt Lisa to drag me back to Edinburgh if I keep ignoring them completely. I don't look over all the messages I've missed, but I do send one of my own:

July 18, 8:18 a.m.
Me: I don't want to talk but I'm alive.

I'll continue to occasionally update them on my status of being alive, but that's all they're getting.

•••

I spend the rest of the day trying to find my art style. Calum said it would take time, so it's not like I expected to have everything figured out over one weekend. I did expect to have *something* figured out, though—even if it was small. Like, maybe my style is graphite pencils, or thin lines, or heavy shading. I would have even been okay with figuring out what my style *isn't*—like that I don't draw backgrounds or give my people facial features. Instead, all I have are a dozen crowded sketchpad pages covered with art that looks like Dad's.

Urgh.

I want to chuck all my work out the window. Instead, I pry myself off my floor bed and stumble into the living room. Maybe a change in scenery will clear my head.

I'm still in pajamas even though it's almost noon—Rose is visiting family and Calum is at work because he's Calum, so I'm alone in the flat with Benji. I haven't seen him all day because I've been curled up in my room, but I find him sitting on the floor next to the coffee table, and he's holding a knife.

Okay, it's just a tiny blade. But when he presses it into the thick paper on the table, I gasp.

"Why are you ruining your art?!" I yell, rushing over and sitting down beside him. Up close, I get a better look at the paper he just destroyed. It's a quick pen drawing of a cat holding a bundle of balloons that . . . aren't actually balloons. They're balls of yarn.

It's adorable. But Benji just cut a line down the cat's side! "Why did you do that?!" I ask, trying to push his hand with the blade away.

He gives me an amused look. "It's a stencil," he explains. "For my street art?"

I frown. "Oh." I obviously know what a stencil is, but I didn't realize people used them for street art. "So you . . . cut a shape out of the paper? And then . . . paint over the hole you created?"

"Essentially." He brings the blade back to the paper and shows me how he makes cuts over the pen marks. "If you cut the whole design out, you'll get a silhouette when you spray-paint. If you make just a few cuts instead, the design will have more definition. I like to start with a solid base and then add layers on top to create shadows and highlights." He nudges a stack of papers with his elbow. They're all copies of the same cat balloon picture, but with different lines cut into each of them.

"Oh," I say. "That's actually cool. Can I watch you do the spray-painting?"

Benji shakes his head. "It's toxic. I can't use it indoors."

"There are a lot of bare buildings outside just asking to be decorated."

"You know perfectly well it's illegal without the proper permits."

I lean forward on my elbows and force my face to stay serious. "It's only illegal if we get caught."

He snorts. "Maisie Clark, who have you been listening to? You should run very far from anyone giving out that sort of life advice."

I blink. It takes him a good five seconds to realize his mistake. When he does, he groans and presses a hand to his forehead. "No, no, I never told you that. I am a *good* influence. I—" He stops, seeming to reconsider. "I at least refuse to be worse than Rose."

I bite back a smile. "She did say she got drunk at a party once and wrote a twenty-page essay about why she's sure Calum's a spy."

Benji's eyes go wide. "She—all right, listen closely. Drinking is bad. Illegal street art is bad. Don't do either of those things, because they are not fun, and even if—hypothetically—they are not entirely un-fun, they are still very bad. Is that our bases covered? Oh, and never listen to a word Rose or I say. That one is very important, as we should not be allowed to say things." He shakes his head. "What will your parents think when—" he cuts off, but it's too late.

There is suddenly water in the air, and it might be tears, and they might be mine. They don't fall—I don't let them—but the now-familiar fury I feel every time I think of home presses against my eyes. "My parents don't get to think anything," I mutter stonily. "Not after what they did."

"You're angry." Benji says it as though it isn't obvious, as though he doesn't feel the same way.

I frown. "You're not?"

He chews at his lip. Eventually he says, "Cal doesn't like dwelling on the past, so I try not to, either."

"Doesn't *that* bother you?" I press. "That there's a whole part of Calum's life he doesn't talk about? I mean, unless he talks about it with you. *Does* he talk about it with you?"

Benji shrugs. "Rarely, but that's all right. Everyone has things they'd rather not speak about. Even you must keep some things private."

I think about it, but . . . I'm a pretty open book. I mean, I even told my dad about the horrific first time I got my period last March and bled all over a chair in the science lab. If I could admit to *that* . . .

But maybe that's a bad example. I don't really find embarrassing things hard to talk about. They sting, but the cuts are shallow. When it comes to things buried deeper . . . maybe Benji has a point. There is at least one thing I haven't told anyone.

Before this summer, I thought I knew who I was. An artist. A sister. A friend. A daughter. But how can I be an artist without my own style, or a sister if my brother shuts me out? How can I be a friend when I can't even get *my* best friend to answer my texts? So much of my confidence came from knowing who I was and who I wanted to be. Now my insides are so jumbled that they don't even look like *mine*.

The room spins—except, not really. I'm the one who's spiraling. I place a hand flat on the coffee table, trying to ground myself before Benji notices.

He's not looking at me, though. His head is tilted, his brows furrowed, like he's thinking hard about what to say next. "The thing is," he says finally, "I'm not even sure if talking about home with Calum would show me things about him that I can't see already. Facts tell you what happened to a person, but not who they've become because of them. I don't need to hear about who Calum was to see who he is now."

He gestures at me and then at himself. "People are more than one thing. We're so many things. We all have—" He grimaces. "Oh, I ruined it. I was going to say we all have layers, but now all that's in my head is the line from *Shrek* about how ogres are like onions, and listen, I know you'll roll your eyes at me in that way you do, but it's a valid point."

I roll my eyes for his benefit, but keep my hair partially in front of my face in case I still look spirally. "What is *with* all the *Shrek*? Aren't you guys too old to be watching kids' movies?"

"Ouch." Benji claps a hand to his heart like I stabbed him. Then he smiles again—softer this time. "Rose and I like to complain when Cal requests it, but it's actually a fantastic film. It has so many . . . layers . . ."

I sigh loudly, but it's more of a breath of relief than a sound of annoyance. Despite the weird *Shrek* obsession in this household, I get what he's saying. When an artist paints someone, they can only capture them at one angle, in one pose. But with just one pose, a good artist can capture a person's entire essence. Although you only see a sliver of them in the finished piece, you can tell who they are at their core.

Before this summer, I couldn't even picture what Calum looked like in my head. Now I have scowling photos of him on my phone—of *us* on my phone. Now I know when he's pretend-angry and that he shockingly doesn't sleep in his suits and that he drove seven hours to see me in Scotland and that he may or may not be a spy. I don't know everything about him, but I do know some things, and some things are so much better than nothing.

My stomach jolts. If I don't need to see every angle of Calum to know who he is, maybe I don't need to see every angle of me to know who *I* am. I'm not just an artist or a friend or a daughter. I am more than one angle. I'm an infinity of angles, so maybe it's okay if I don't have them all figured out.

"I understand," I say finally. "Not about why you think *Shrek* is a masterpiece, but the other thing."

Benji looks surprised. "Really? Well . . . brilliant! Maybe I should pursue teaching. Clearly I've a secret knack for it."

"I thought you were studying to be an imaginary number. You should probably stick to that."

Benji grabs his chest again. "Brutal."

"You could teach art," I amend, turning my attention back to his stencils. "Actually . . ." My mind flips back to the question I've been struggling with over the past couple of days. "Could you tell me how you found your art style?" Even if I'm more than my art, that doesn't mean it isn't still an important part of me. It's one of the angles I'm most desperate to figure out.

Benji looks at his cat drawing and cocks his head to the side. "Oh. Er . . . I don't think I ever went looking for it, to be honest. One day I glanced down and it was sort of just there."

I groan loudly. Benji looks alarmed, so I wave a hand and mutter, "Calum practically said the same thing. I know it takes time to find your own style, but *how much time?*"

Benji nudges his stencil with a finger. "I don't think my art started looking distinctly mine for several years, but I did notice a difference when—" He throws up a hand. "Oh! I have an idea. Hang on." He jumps to his feet and darts out of the living room. I blink hard, jarred by his abruptness.

He returns a moment later with an iPad. "Have you ever tried digital art?" he asks.

I shake my head. I always liked the idea, but it's kind of intimidating. It would almost be like having to learn to draw all over again.

Wait a minute . . .

My heartbeat picks up. Isn't learning to draw again—in my own style—kind of the point? I look at the iPad with more interest. "Isn't it difficult?"

Benji swipes the lock screen open and clicks on a drawing app. "There are a lot of advanced features, but you don't have to learn them all at once. It's quite simple to do a basic sketch or painting." He shows me how touch sensitive the stylus is, how easy it is to erase and undo any lines I don't like, and how to create layers so when I paint on one, it doesn't affect what I've done on the others.

"I did a lot of digital art when I was younger," he explains as I play with the stylus. "But when I started to branch out in uni, that's when I really began to learn what worked for me and what didn't. Maybe dabbling in a medium you've never tried before will help you find your style."

I glance up at him. "That's a good idea."

He grins. "Look at me, being helpful twice in one day. Miracles *do* exist."

It's so hard not to roll my eyes this time.

Benji goes back to his stencils and leaves me to experiment with the iPad on the couch. There are so many features—more than I can imagine how to use or what to do with. But there are also some immediate pros to working digitally. The undo button is amazing. It's hard to erase on a real piece of paper without there being at least a little bit of residue, but on the iPad, I can wipe a line completely clean with the simple press of a button. I can also switch between paint and ink brushes with zero effort. There's a blending tool, there are gradient backgrounds, I can add text and photos, and I can zoom in and out and—

The list is endless.

I don't notice the time passing. Rose gets home at five, and I jump when the door slams. Reluctantly, I hold the iPad out to Benji as he gets up to help her make dinner. "Digital art is really cool. Thanks for letting me try it out."

"You like it?" he asks.

I nod. "There's so much . . ." It takes me a second to find the right word. "Potential. It's just one screen and a pen, but you can do . . . *everything.*" I can't help the awe that seeps into my voice.

Benji assesses my face. "In that case . . ." He gently pushes the iPad back at me. "Why don't you hold on to it while you're in London? I rarely use it these days. I'm sure you'll get more out of it than me."

I stare at him, disbelieving. *"Really?"*

His lips quirk up. "Sure."

It takes all my effort not to hug the iPad to my chest. "Thank you," I breathe, eyes wide.

He holds up a finger as though trying to press pause on my excitement. "I do have one request, however. If you are to keep it all summer."

I grip the iPad tighter, scared I'm going to lose it as soon as I've gained it. "Okay?"

His eyes grow very serious. "Once you become an incredibly famous artist, you must promise to design a statue of me to be placed in Hyde Park."

I blink. "Is that all?"

He considers. "Well, if you've already designed the one, I wouldn't say no to a dozen more. I would like to have a different pose in each, as well as a different outfit. At least one must include a cape. If you cannot guarantee a cape, I'll have to take the iPad back immediately."

This time I really do hug the screen, pressing it hard against my ribs like I can absorb its contents into my body. "I'll see what I can do."

Sometimes People Aren't Awful,
Part Two

I spend the rest of the evening experimenting with the iPad, but for some reason, my talk with Benji about how you can know someone without knowing every little thing about them keeps making me think of Alicia.

I got angry at her for being distant and not answering my texts these past few weeks—but no, I'm angry at my parents. With Alicia . . .

I was scared.

Lately it's felt like we've been slipping back into how things were before she promised she wasn't trying to push me away. But it wasn't fair of me to blame her for our distance this summer. Ever since I got to London, *I'm* the one who's been ignoring *her*.

My stomach jolts at the realization.

Alicia texted and texted, asking if I was around to talk. I kept telling her I'd get back to her when I was free, but I never did.

Why did I send her those nasty texts?

Will I ever stop being so selfish?

Before I can overthink it, I grab my phone and press her number on FaceTime.

She answers on the first ring.

"Hi," I say quietly.

"Hi." Her face is flushed, her freckles standing out more than usual against the pink splotches on her skin. At first I think she's angry—which, yeah. I'd be angry at me, too. But the harder I look . . . I frown, bringing the screen closer to my face.

"Have you been crying?"

Alicia shakes her head, but her eyes are red and puffy, and she's never been a good liar.

"Alicia . . ."

"Sorry . . ." she mutters, swiping the back of her hand over her eyes. "You caught me at a weird time. It's been a week."

My stomach drops again. It would be one thing if Alicia ignored my texts out of anger, but if it wasn't even that, if it was because she was sad . . .

"What happened?" I ask. "Something with your parents?"

She shakes her head.

"Tennis?"

Another shake.

"Rowan?"

Her face wavers.

Oh.

"Did you . . . fight, or something?" When she doesn't respond to that, I ask what I think she's not saying, "Did you break up?"

Her eyes fill with tears. She hides her mouth behind her arm as though it will muffle the words that come tumbling out. "It was just . . . from movies, to food, to dates, we couldn't agree on *anything*," she mumbles. "And then, on the camping trip, we realized we should just . . . that it was just . . ." She sniffles and wipes her nose with the back of her hand. "I'm sorry I didn't answer when you said something intense happened. I was trying to be there for you, but then Rowan and I were a disaster, and then I was trying to fix things, and then you were mad at me, and I guess I should have told you what was going on but I didn't want to bother you with my stuff when you had your own stuff and—"

"Alicia, no. I'm so sorry. I should have checked in with you the way you've been doing with me. I should have—"

"I don't blame you," she counters. "I mean, yeah. I was angry that you kept blowing me off. But it's not like I didn't get it—you're in London with your long-lost brother. That's huge—"

"And you were in your first relationship! That's just as huge."

Alicia lowers her head, and my chest aches. When did things become so complicated? Alicia and I have had the same schedule since kindergarten: walk to school, go to class, hang out at my or her house, repeat. We essentially shared a life, but now I have family stuff she's not a part of, and she was in a relationship that had nothing to do with me, and . . .

"I'm not used to being so far away from you." It's difficult to say that out loud. But when I do, her head snaps up.

"Yes." She nods. "Every time something funny happened this summer, I'd turn to laugh with you, and it would take another second to remember you weren't there."

"You can text me the funny things," I say earnestly. "And the sad things. And the random things. Even if I can't always respond, I'll read them. I promise."

She nods again, more slowly this time. "You, too. You can text me all the things, too."

The conversation fades to silence. But maybe that's okay. It's like with Calum, isn't it? Even if Alicia and I aren't talking with each other 24/7 anymore, even if we don't share every moment of our lives, that doesn't mean we can't still be close. Our friendship might require more effort than it did when we were little, but that's okay. It's worth it.

Alicia's lips turn up in a tentative smile. "Does this mean we're not going to fight? When you called, I thought I was going to yell at you. But I'd honestly rather skip that part. I hate fighting with you even more than I hate tennis."

I match her smile and hold out a hand, as if there aren't a screen and three thousand miles between us. "I missed you."

She pretends to complete the handshake through the phone. "Missed you, too."

•••

Alicia and I talk for a long time, but not about Rowan or my parents. It feels good to talk about easy things, to pretend for a little while that there is nothing deeper. She tells me how boring it's been to walk German and Shepherd without me in the evenings, but that she's been amusing herself by narrating their lives like a nature documentary.

"And then German pranced through the tall grass, one paw in front of the other, a sight of dignified beauty and grace . . ."

I tell her about the finance museum with Calum, and about how Benji lent me his iPad in exchange for my promise to design a statue of him.

"I actually *did* start sketching the statue. I'm pretty sure he'll pee his pants when I show him . . ."

After some nagging, I even get Alicia to show me a photo of her tennis class. She's holding her racquet like it's a dead animal someone forced her to pick up, and the look of disgust on her face is so intense that I laugh for a solid five minutes.

The easy talk can't go on forever, though. Not when there are harder conversations under the surface. I knew we would have to address them eventually, but I didn't expect them to bubble up so soon.

". . . weird walking by the Glenna's workshop and seeing your dad inside without you," Alicia is saying. "I hate watching him pack up equipment. It makes it feel so real."

That's all it takes for the air to rush from my lungs. "He's packing up equipment?" I repeat. "Why?"

Alicia frowns. "I mean, now that your parents have decided to close the shop, they've got to pack at some point. That's what you wanted to talk about the other day, right? The intense thing that happened? I'm so sorry. Mom only told me this morning. If I'd known sooner—"

Alicia tilts her head, or maybe I do. Tilt mine, I mean. Do I tilt?

I'm falling. I'm falling, but I'm sitting.

The room is spinning.

Am I spinning?

Maybe I should breathe.

I can't breathe.

Alicia brings her face right up to the camera, eyes wide with concern. "Maisie, did you . . . not *know*?"

My chest is moving very fast.

I gulp for air.

I gulp again.

"When?" I finally manage to croak out. "How? *What?*"

Alicia gives me another very concerned look, but says, "Mom told me your parents got really close to finding a new investor. There's an organization in New York that specializes in funding small businesses, but in the end they rejected Glenna's because they didn't think there was a big enough market of people buying traditional portraits. There isn't time to find another investor before the Knightley funding runs out, and although your parents can afford to keep the shop open for a while longer, they'd be losing money the whole time. So they decided to close it down now . . ." She trails off, her frown deepening. "They really didn't tell you?"

"I haven't talked to them in a while," I say numbly. I think I'm in shock. Today is July 18th. We don't lose the funding until August 1st. I was supposed to have two more weeks to save Glenna's.

How could Mom and Dad do this without telling me?

Is it their way of punishing me for ignoring their calls?

Fury blooms in my chest, but it just as quickly fizzles out. I'm tired of being angry. It takes so much effort.

"Why haven't you talked to your parents in a while?" Alicia asks after I don't say anything.

I shake my head. "It's complicated."

She leans her chin on her hand. "I'm listening."

It's those two words that do it. Even though I'm exhausted, when I open my mouth, everything comes pouring out. I tell her about Calum. About my parents. About my video project and my plan to save Glenna's. Alicia listens the whole time and curses at all the right moments, and by the time I finish, she's on her back in the grass with the phone raised above her head. I faintly hear German and Shepherd barking at each other in the distance.

"Anyway, things with Calum are good, but I don't know what to do about Mom and Dad," I finish. "And now all the weeks I spent working on this video don't even matter, and I'm just—" I don't know what I am. I wave a frantic hand through the air as if that will explain it to both of us.

Alicia chews on her cheek. After a moment she says, "I'm not sure what to do about your parents. They . . . what they did to Calum is messed up, and it's awful they never told you why he left home. But about Glenna's . . . You have a way to save it, right? You're making a video?"

"Yeah, but if Mom and Dad already decided to close the shop—"

"Just because your parents gave up doesn't mean you have to!"

I blink. We technically still have two weeks to convince Knightley to renew the Glenna's funding. If I finish my video and bring it to Calum's office before then . . .

It probably won't work.

There's a chance it could.

An ember lights in my stomach. For the first time in a while, the warmth inside me doesn't stem from rage. "I have to go."

Alicia grins. "Yeah, you do!"

I end the call, grab my laptop, and open iMovie all in one motion. I have all the footage I need to finish the project: the only thing left is the editing. If I work really hard, I think I can cobble something together by morning.

I pull my blankets close and get to work.

Don't Lock Yourself Out of Your Own House On Purpose

I decide that the best way to bring my video project to Calum's office is to do it without telling anyone.

I obviously can't tell Calum because he doesn't want to be involved with anything related to Glenna's. I can't tell Benji or Rose, either, because there's no way they'll let me go behind my brother's back—not when I'm essentially planning on storming his workplace and causing a scene. So on Monday morning, after Calum leaves for work and Benji and Rose are getting ready for class, I don't get out of bed.

Rose walks over to my mattress and gently prods my shoulder. "We've got to leave in twenty minutes."

I shake my head. "I can't do math today."

"Are you feeling all right?"

"Just tired. I haven't really had a break since I got to the UK."

Rose looks at me, considering. "We have been running you ragged, haven't we? Unfortunately, Calum's at work—shocker—and I'm also out most of the day. Benji has class until half five—"

"I don't need anyone to stay with me. I'm pretty sure I can manage not to set the flat on fire while you're gone."

Rose hesitates. "It's not that I don't trust you, but you're not *my* sister. If something happens because I left you on your own—"

"I'm almost *thirteen*." The anger that's become a part of my body over the last few weeks makes its way into my voice. "I'm not a child. Why can't you just leave me alone?"

She flinches, and I feel awful. I'm not mad at her. I'm mad at my parents, but they're not here to yell at. "Sorry." I pack as much sincerity into the word as possible. "I didn't sleep well, and I haven't had any time to myself in weeks, and I just . . . I want to be alone." My voice cracks slightly at the end of the sentence. I thought this whole "I'm tired" thing was purely a lie to get her to leave me by myself, but I've barely slept in days. The tears that come to my eyes are only a little bit forced.

Rose sits back on her heels. "I get it." She pats my arm again. "It's important to take time for yourself. I suppose you can stay home, but if you need anything—I know you're capable of handling yourself—but if anything happens, you have my number. Don't be afraid to use it."

Some of the tension in my chest releases. I nod, curling back under my blankets.

Rose points a finger at me that I think is supposed to be threatening, but she's wearing those fuzzy pink socks again, and they really take away her authority. "Give me your word you won't leave the flat. If Calum finds out you were wandering London on your own . . ."

"I promise."

I hate that I've become so good at lying.

●●●

The first thing I do after Rose and Benji leave is open Google Maps on my phone. I won't have cell service once I leave the flat, but if I type in the directions while I still have Wi-Fi, I'll be able to keep following the little arrow on the screen. The only problem is if I make one wrong turn, the map won't reload and my directions will be useless.

My heart is practically beating out of my chest, but I try to embrace the fear. I let it quicken my pulse and clear my brain. I'm an almost teenager. I'm fully capable of navigating this city on my own without Wi-Fi. I can totally convince a corporation to reinvest in my family's business.

I can do this I can do this I can do this.

Deep breath in. Out. I open the front door, and when it closes behind me, the click of the lock sets my nerves on fire. There's no turning back now—literally. I've never gone out on my own before, so I don't have a key to the flat.

I try not to think too hard about that.

Walking to the tube station is easy. It's the same one I take with Rose and Benji to get to the university, so I find it with no trouble. And because I've taken the tube so often, I have my own Oyster card. I pull it out of my wallet—which also contains two sticks of stale gum and the emergency money Mom gave me before I left home—and press the card against the scanner. The little gate swoops open, and I'm shoved through and swept into a crowd of commuters.

According to my screenshotted directions, I have to take the Circle Line to Liverpool Street Station. I usually take the Central Line with Rose and Benji, so when I get to the turn in the tunnels we usually take, I pause to figure out which direction I'm supposed to go in today. The crowd surges, pushing me this way and that, and I'm not tall enough to read the signs, and suddenly I'm being forced into a tunnel and onto a random train platform, and the line says "Piccadilly" instead of "Circle," and there are too many people behind me, and I can't turn back—

I hear the rumble of a train but don't see when it pulls into the station. I'm too short, and there are too many people, and I'm being shoved forward again, and *this is the wrong train, I can't get on this train*—

I turn and elbow against the current, shoving away from the train doors. A woman huffs as my arm catches her in the side; an old man side-eyes me as my toes land on his. But I keep pushing, and I'm sweating buckets, and I can't breathe because of the crowd and the heat and the—

I break free of the people and almost fall to my knees in the now-empty tunnel. Before I can catch my breath or cry or even *think*, I realize I need to move, *now*, before the people coming off the train catch up to me and I'm stuck in the same mess as before. I race down the tunnels, looking for anything that says "Circle" or "Liverpool," and God, there's a whole city above me and hundreds of footsteps on either side of me, and this is starting to feel very claustrophobic and—*Circle*.

The yellow train map has arrows pointing in two directions. The rumble of new footsteps creeps closer as I frantically try to figure out whether to turn right or left. *Liverpool Street Liverpool Street Liverpool Str*—

I find it and turn left onto the platform, gasping and fanning myself with my Oyster card and pleading the train arrives before the station fills up again. Of course, the second I think this, the platform swarms. I'm toward the front of the crowd, so I assume I'll be saved from all these people when the train pulls in. But when the doors open, the cars are just as packed as the platform. I shove my way inside, and suddenly I'm standing with my face half an inch from someone's back and my back half an inch from someone's stomach, and I have nothing to hold on to as the train lurches forward, and I'm too short to read the sign telling me how many stops until mine, and I think I might be panicking, but there's nowhere to go and nothing I can do, and—

I'm not sure when I start crying. Maybe I've been crying since I first swiped my Oyster card; maybe the tears didn't fall until I stepped onto the train. But the next thing I know, I'm wiping snot on my bare arm because I don't have a tissue, and instead of asking what's wrong or trying to help, the people around me glower in disgust and turn away.

I need Calum. That's the first thought that jumps into my head. The second is: *I need to get off this train.*

I don't know how many stops the train has gone. I don't know if I passed Liverpool Street or if I'm jumping off way too early. All I know is when the doors open, I'm elbowing my way off the platform and up the stairs and into fresh air.

I don't stop to figure out where I am. As soon as I get outside, I lean against a wall and force my shaking fingers to turn on my emergency phone service. Then I call Calum.

He picks up on the fourth ring. "Maisie, I'm running into a meeting. Really can't talk—"

"You have to come get me."

"What? Where are you?"

"I don't know. The tube was hot and crowded, and I had to get off, and I'm not supposed to be using my phone but—"

"Where are Benji and Rose?"

"I don't know. At school. I was supposed to stay in the flat, but I wanted to come to your office and—"

Calum curses. "You're *alone*? What were you thinking? I *told* you not to go anywhere by yourself—"

"I know, I know! I'm sorry. I'm sorry."

Calum sighs. I can almost picture him running a hand through his hair, messing up the dark waves. "Where are you?"

"I don't know. I had to get off the train, so I did, and now I'm—it's so crowded and I'm—"

"Stay calm," he says. "Look around. Are you still near the tube station?"

"Yeah," I mutter, feeling ridiculous that I didn't think of this before. I turn around, and the name of the station is printed right behind me. "Yeah, I'm at Blackfriars."

"Okay. Do you see any cafés nearby? Starbucks? Anything like that?"

I look up and down the street, spinning in a slow circle. "There's one across from me. Pret A . . . something. It looks French."

"Great," Calum says. "Go in and wait for me. It's going to take me about twenty minutes to get to you. Okay?"

I nod. "Yeah."

After he hangs up, I'm a little calmer. I mean, I'm still terri-fied and sweating so much that there can't be any water left in my body, but I'm not alone anymore. I'm not going to die on the streets of London without anyone knowing.

I walk into the café. I never thought air-conditioning would make me cry happy tears, but it does. It's more crowded in here than I want it to be, so I find an empty spot toward the back and slump into a chair, put my elbows on the cold metal table, and bury my head in my arms.

I don't know how long I sit like this. I guess it must be around twenty minutes, because suddenly a low voice is saying "Maisie?" and I'm jumping up and grabbing my brother around the waist and sobbing into his expensive collared shirt.

He stiffens, but after a moment he wraps his arms around me, pressing me into him even though I'm definitely wrinkling his suit. We stay like that for several beats—by the desperate way I'm holding him, the people around us probably think we're re-uniting for the first time in years.

I guess we are.

My Brother Is Famous?!

A few minutes later, Calum and I are settled in the café. I'm chugging a bottle of freezing water and trying to resist pouring some on my face. Calum bites into half of the chocolate croissant we decided to split, watching me carefully. I assume he's going to launch into a lecture about how irresponsible it was for me to leave the flat on my own. Instead, he says, "When I first got to London, I panicked on the tube at least once a week. It's so hot and crowded down there. Absolute nightmare."

I blink. "*You* don't like the tube? Really?"

"Why do you sound surprised?"

"I just . . . I thought you loved everything about London. Isn't that why you came to work here instead of staying in Edinburgh?"

Calum's mouth splits into a smile. I've seen him smile before, but not like this. Even though he's all dressed up in his suit and stuffy atmosphere, he suddenly looks familiar. When his lips spread, his cheeks get all fat, and his nose crinkles just like mine does. I'm so taken aback that I almost forget what we're talking about. "You think I'm happy here?" he asks, like the question is absurd.

"Well . . . yes?"

Calum shakes his head slightly as he bites into his croissant again. "When Mom and Dad . . . when I moved to Scotland, I wasn't exactly thrilled. But Aunt Lisa's amazing, and Edinburgh started to feel like home. When it came time to apply to universities, I wanted to stay near Aunt Lisa. I would have, if I hadn't been so focused on moving to a bigger city. I thought if I got a fancy job and made a lot of money in London, I'd be able to travel, see the world. But the truth is, I've been here for four years and I haven't really left. I didn't have the money to travel while I was in university, and I don't have the time now because my job is so intense."

"Do you even like your job?"

He shrugs. "I don't hate it."

"That's not the same as liking it. You should do something you're passionate about! You should—"

Calum raises his eyebrows. "We're not here to talk about me. Maisie, why did you take the tube by yourself?"

"I—" It's too late to come up with a plausible lie. Also, I miss telling the truth. "I want to show Knightley Corporations my video project," I say quietly. "The one I made to save Glenna's. I know they'll probably laugh in my face, but—"

Calum frowns. "I thought you gave up on that. Benji said you've not filmed anything with him in weeks."

"I didn't *give up*. I was angry at Mom and Dad, so I stopped working on it. But Alicia called me yesterday and said . . . she said it's over. Mom and Dad are closing the shop at the end of the month, and I—I can't let them do that without at least trying to save it. I *have* to at least try—" My voice breaks. I look away.

"I thought you wanted to find your own art style."

"Can't I do both? The shop . . . it's Mom and Dad's, yeah, but it's also mine. It's Aunt Lisa's. It's yours. At some point or another, we all put parts of ourselves into it. I don't want to lose a part of me—a part of us—if I don't have to!" I scrub my hands across my face. "My video—"

Calum's voice is low when he cuts me off. "It's not going to work."

I bristle. "I know it's a long shot, but I've been working really hard, and it's good and—"

"Even if it's the most spectacular video in the world, it's not going to convince Knightley to reinvest in Glenna's. The funding for small businesses? It doesn't exist anymore. They cut the entire department last month."

I don't think he's trying to be mean, but his words stab my already open wounds. "I have to try." I'm on the edge of anger again. "Even if it's impossible, I can't not try. It's *Glenna's.*"

"I'm not telling you to give up." Calum's fingers tighten around the paper his croissant is wrapped in. "If I really thought showing your project to the investment department would make a difference, I'd have offered to bring you myself."

I stare at him. "You're not mad?"

One side of his mouth turns up. "I wish you hadn't gone behind my back, but I know why you did. And to be honest, I thought you were going to try this ages ago. I'm only surprised you waited so long."

My mouth drops a little. Am I really that obvious?

"You're not obvious," he says, because apparently he's a mind reader as well as a spy. "Well, I wouldn't call you subtle. But . . ." He points a finger at his head and then at mine. "We're more similar than you realize."

He might be right. I mean, on the outside he's an awkward nerd with a boring job, whereas I'm awesome, but there are times when we're oddly in sync.

Calum gives me a long look. "I've been thinking about what you said in Kensington Gardens. About how you love Glenna's because it shaped you into who you are. I didn't get to keep a lot of the people or places that shaped me, so I . . . don't want you to lose something this important if you don't have to." He pulls out his phone and starts typing.

I glance up at him, then down at his phone. "Is that the end of the conversation?"

He waves a hand. "Obviously not. Hang on a minute."

I give him an exasperated look that he doesn't see because he's focused on his phone.

"Okay," he says after way longer than a minute. He turns his phone for me to see. There's an Instagram page open on his screen. Not the Instagram with no picture that he uses to stalk me with: a different one. It's called "Dottie," and the profile photo is a cartoonish drawing of a green giraffe. It looks like most of the photos posted on the account are drawings of the giraffe and a few other animals. A lot of the pictures include text bubbles the way comics and graphic novels do.

"When we were in the park, I mentioned I have a web comic. This is my Instagram for it," Calum explains.

"Oh." Suddenly, something clicks. I know that giraffe. Everything in Calum's room in Crescent Valley is exactly the same as it was when he lived at home—his gray and black plaid comforter, the bare walls, the green rug. Even though it must have been clear pretty quickly that he wasn't coming back, Mom and Dad never cleared out his stuff. But the giraffe was special. It's the only thing Mom moved.

I asked her about it a few years ago, when I saw it on her nightstand. "You know how you bring Poppy every time you sleep at a friend's house or we stay at a hotel?" Mom pointed at the purple penguin I've had since I was born. "It's the same with Calum and Dottie. Dad and I don't have anything from our childhoods that still gives us meaning. We wanted the two of you to have something to always remind you of home, of us, which is why we bought you those stuffed animals when you were born."

Calum didn't take Dottie with him to the UK, but he held on to a part of her with his comic. I guess even though home is painful for him, there are parts he wants to keep.

He wants to keep Dottie, and—

Well. He wants to keep me.

"It's cool," I say, scrolling through the pictures. I can't tell what the comic is about just from the Instagram, but I really like the drawings. "Why are you showing me this, though?"

Calum moves my hand off the screen and scrolls back to the top of the page. He points at his follower count, which I didn't notice before.

100,000. Calum has 100,000 followers.

"Um. What?" I blink to make sure I'm seeing correctly. "Is that . . . real?"

He nods, then closes Instagram and opens Twitter. His handle is @GreenDottie, and he has nearly 75,000 followers.

Before I can gasp dramatically, he opens Safari. The webpage on his screen looks like the official site for his comic, but it's on admin mode, and a graph is pulled up. It shows a bunch of numbers, and it takes me a second to realize this is how many views his website gets per month. The average is 500,000.

"What?" I say again. "You're like . . . famous?"

"Definitely not." Calum shudders. "Dottie's anonymous. Only a few people know I run the accounts, and besides, five hundred thousand hardly counts for famous these days."

He sets down his phone and steeples his fingers. "My idea is that we post your video on my website and social medias and start a Patreon account. For a monthly fee, people can sign up to support Glenna's in exchange for some art done by you. I've seen you working on the iPad—I know you've only just started, but you're talented, Maisie. I think people would be interested if you decided to offer digital portraits. You'll still need an investor, of course, but this should buy you time. If nothing else, it's more practical than coming into my office to yell at a department that no longer exists."

I'm kind of speechless. It never occurred to me that Calum's web comic might be popular. Not because he's a bad artist—it's just, 500,000 views a month? The number is so big I can't really grasp it. And more than that: I never thought Calum would offer to help with Glenna's.

I look at his phone, which sits between us on the table. We needed a miracle, and that's essentially what he's offering me. But . . .

"You don't have to do this." It's so hard to say the words. It's even harder to push his phone back toward him. "Don't do this for me."

Calum shakes his head. "It's not for you. I mean, it is. But Glenna's is also where I fell in love with art. Like you said, Mom and Dad might run the shop, but all of us, back to Grandma Glenna, put parts of ourselves into it. Besides, I wouldn't have started my web comic if it weren't for Glenna's. It was my spite project when I felt like my art didn't fit with the rest of our house, and look at it now." He shoots me a small smile. "Thank you for telling me I don't have to do this. You're sweet to say that. But I wouldn't have offered if I weren't sure."

My mouth is still open in shock. I want to hug him again, but I'm not that brave. Instead I mutter, "I changed my mind."

His eyebrows dimple. "About what?"

"Don't take this the wrong way, but you're . . ." Urgh. I can't believe I'm about to admit this to his face. "You're not . . . completely uncool."

He frowns and leans closer. "Sorry, it's so loud in here. What did you say?"

I squirt my water bottle at him. He jumps back, nearly knocking over his chair. "I'm not repeating it."

He smiles that same smile from earlier, where his cheeks get big. "Come on." He nods at the door. "I'll take you home."

"Don't you have to go back to your office?"

"I've worked overtime every day for the last two years. My boss can do without me for one afternoon. Besides, we have to start on your video launch. It's not going to be easy to pull off."

If the hope in my chest balloons any further, I'm going to fly away.

Things Were Going So Well

The next few days are a mess in the best way. Calum tells Benji and Rose about Glenna's, and our project becomes all-hands-on-deck.

I spend hours on the streets with Benji, finding and interviewing new people to make art for so that we can add a little more substance into my video. While we run around, Calum creates the Patreon account and drafts a message about why Glenna's is important to us. We'll post it along with my video, and it will hopefully gain more attention for the shop.

Rose has apparently been downplaying her artistic abilities, because I find out she's great at graphic design. Calum and I assign her to renovate the Twitter I made for Glenna's, and she creates a gorgeous profile picture the shop can use as a logo.

Even Alicia pitches in. She sneaks outside my house every day to see if my parents have met with more investors or cleared more equipment from the shop. So far it's a no on both counts, which . . . I wouldn't say that's *good*, but at least Mom and Dad haven't sent a wrecking ball into the workshop or anything.

As things begin to come together, a new thought takes form in my head. Alicia said the New York investor rejected Glenna's because they didn't think there were enough people who want to buy traditional portraits. At its core, Glenna's is a portrait shop. I don't want to change that—it wouldn't be Glenna's if we did. But . . . Calum's idea that I should offer digital portraits as an incentive for people to support the shop lit my imagination on fire. Even though my days now revolve around my video project, I'm still spending hours every night using Benji's iPad to practice digital art. I wouldn't say I'm amazing at it, but I think I could be one day. I'm excited at the thought of practicing and practicing and slowly getting better.

What if we added digital portraits into Glenna's official products? They'd be much cheaper than our oil paintings, would be quicker to make, and could be used for more things. Like, you could buy one for a social media profile photo, or as a gift for a friend, or we could even put the portraits on sweatshirts or enamel pins or metal prints or something. My heart beats faster just thinking about all the possibilities.

On Thursday evening, as we're putting the final touches on the project before the launch, I ask, "Is it done?"

Calum nods. "I still think we should wait until Sunday to go live, as that's when I publish my comic every week. But for now, I think this calls for pizza."

"Pizza?" Rose shouts from somewhere to my right.

"Pizza?" Benji echoes her enthusiasm.

Over the past week, we've inhabited different spaces in the living room. Calum's notes take up the table, Benji's paint and research for potential art locations cover the couch, Rose has made a home for herself on the floor by the window, and I'm half-buried under papers near the TV. When Calum mentions pizza and everyone cheers, I can't find them in all the clutter even though I know exactly where they are.

Rose emerges from under a pile of sticky notes and slips on a granola wrapper as she gets to her feet. "Instead of cleaning this disaster flat together, I think we should put it to a vote," she says, flicking another wrapper off the couch. "Whoever gets the most votes has to do all the cleaning by themselves. Agreed?"

"Sure," I say.

Benji nods.

"Absolutely not," says Calum.

Rose widens her eyes at him. "Why do you always ruin the fun?"

"Because the three of you will obviously vote for me."

"I would never." Benji places a hand over his heart.

"Of course you will." Calum kicks a stack of paper in his direction.

Rose grins. "You'll never know unless we vote."

Calum walks to the door. "You can figure this out on your own. I'm getting pizza."

Rose scrambles after him. "I suppose The Great Flat Debate can wait."

We walk outside, and Calum freezes. It happens so quickly that Rose smacks into him and Benji smacks into her and I smack into both of them. We all stumble; after Rose catches herself on the doorframe and moves out of the way, I see why my brother stopped short.

Mom and Dad.

They're here.

In front of us.

I freeze.

I don't know how they found Calum's flat. I don't know how they knew we'd be home. But I do know one thing: they're here because of me.

"Calum?" I don't actually hear his name, but I see it on Mom's lips. Even though she obviously knew he would be here, she looks shocked to see him. Dad grabs Mom's wrist, like he suddenly needs support to stand. Mom actually brings a hand to her mouth like someone overacting in a movie.

Calum looks at them. He runs a hand through his hair. Then, without a word, he turns sharply and walks back inside.

"Cal—" Benji begins, but the door slams, cutting him off. He runs after him.

"What's going on?" Rose asks, but there's something in her tone that tells me she already knows.

I confirm it for her. "Our parents."

Everyone is frozen. I thought Mom and Dad would try to chase after Calum, but they don't. They just stare at the closed door. I see a hundred emotions on their faces, but they flicker past too quickly for me to decipher.

"Do you want me to stay?" Rose asks quietly.

I hesitate. It's kind of nice having someone else here as a witness. At the same time, whatever is about to happen is between me and my parents. And Rose keeps glancing toward the flat; she probably wants to make sure Calum is all right.

I shake my head. "Thanks, but you can go."

For a moment, there's no movement. Then Rose's feet shuffle backward. The door opens, and I feel the thump in my chest when it closes.

I'm alone.

My anger at my parents had faded to a background throb over the past week, but now it's white hot again and steaming across my vision. "Why are you here?"

Mom blinks, like she's only just noticing me. "How could we not be here?" she snaps after a pause. "You've not returned our calls in weeks! You're in a different *country* in a huge *city*, and we were worried *sick*—"

"I texted you, didn't I? Even though I didn't want to. I made sure you knew I was okay." Despite the fury pulsing through my body, a hint of guilt works its way into my chest. Even though Mom said she and Dad could afford to send me to Scotland for the summer, I doubt we should be throwing more money at plane tickets right now. But because I wasn't answering their calls, they spent thousands of dollars to cross the ocean and left the shop in the middle of a crisis.

Dad steps toward me. He's paler than normal, and there are dark circles under his eyes. "You are allowed to be angry, Maisie. But sending a two-word text once a week is not enough of a check-in. Besides," he adds when I open my mouth to retort, "we have some news. I didn't want to tell you over text, and since you weren't answering our calls . . ."

"Glenna's." The realization smacks me in the face. "You came here to tell me Glenna's is closing." I thought they kept that information from me as a punishment, but it's the opposite. They know how much the shop means to me, so they wanted to tell me in person. I hate the wave of homesickness that hits me out of nowhere. I hate that, despite everything, the kindness of the gesture makes me realize how much I've *missed* them.

Mom falters. "You already know about Glenna's?"

"Alicia told me. You didn't have to come all the way here just to—"

Mom shakes her head. "Things have been so tense, Piseag. We wanted to see you. To talk face-to-face. We know you . . . these past few weeks, we know you haven't been okay."

That brings my anger right back to the surface. "So you were willing to fly all the way across the ocean because I'm a little upset, but when Calum was upset *at home*—" I falter. "Hang on—how are you even here? Calum never gave you his phone number. How do you know where he lives?"

Dad hesitates. He glances at Mom. Her lips tighten, and after a moment she says, "His boyfriend's Facebook profile is public. He posts a lot of photos, and there are several that include details of the outside of their flat. The street name is visible on one, the building number on another. We never intended to invade Calum's privacy, but . . ." She shakes her head. "We needed to reach you, Maisie. For safety reasons, but also because now that we're closing the shop, we need you home. If we'd simply texted, you wouldn't have gotten on the plane. Don't deny it—we all know you wouldn't have."

They're wrong. Not about the plane, but about the fact that they thought this was the best way to contact me. There were other ways that wouldn't have involved invading my brother's privacy. Off the top of my head: Mom could have asked Aunt Lisa to come talk to me instead of *flying all the way to London*. I cross my arms over my chest and say that last part out loud.

Mom shakes her head. "I did think this through, Maisie. I didn't want to put Lisa at an imposition by asking her to come all the way to London. She has her shop to run, after all. And although you weren't answering our calls, you texted every so often, which meant I knew you were seeing at least some of our messages. When we arrived, I planned to ask you to meet us alone at the café at the end of the road. I didn't account for the fact that the taxi would let us out too far down the block or that we would run into you before I could text. I should have taken into consideration that things might go wrong, but I did try to do this painlessly. I did not want to impose on Calum—"

"Then why were you going through Benji's Facebook?"

Mom stiffens. "I . . . there was never any agenda, Maisie. I occasionally look through his photos because they are the only way for me to see Calum without Calum having to see me. I miss him. I miss him very much."

I flinch. I'm trying so hard to stay angry, but the more we talk, the more I just feel sad. "You didn't listen to him." I hate that my voice cracks. "You were hurting him, and he told you, and you didn't listen. Why didn't you listen?"

Mom is standing the way she always does: shoulders back, chin up, not a hair out of place. But the posture is usually effortless on her, and it's not right now. Her body's shaking. I've never seen Mom shake before. "I knew he wasn't happy at home," she says, very quietly. "I knew I was the one making him unhappy.

But when he told me as much, I thought . . . I thought he was being a teenager, yelling as teenagers do. I didn't think about the message I was sending when I told him to hide his relationship. I didn't realize how it implied I was saying there was a part of him that shouldn't exist."

She closes her eyes. All the fight she came here with seems to have drained away. "Back then . . . even just six years ago, it was harder. For people to be themselves. There were a few incidents in and around Crescent Valley, and I was scared. I was terrified something would happen to him. But . . . he was sixteen. Not an adult by any means, but old enough to have his own opinions about his life. He asked me to listen. I didn't. I regret it every day."

I look down. Mom was scared, so she let her heart make her decisions for her. I get it. I know how easy it is to think with your feelings. But like Rose told me: Brains are important, too.

I glance at Dad. He's not trying to stand tall like Mom is. The longer this conversation goes on, the more he shrinks into himself. He's so quiet. I hope he knows that's harmful, too.

He notices me watching him and closes his eyes. "When I paint, I always know what to say," he murmurs finally. "I used to think that was enough, that I could show my feelings instead of stating them. But sometimes words are necessary. I wish I had learned that sooner."

A scream bubbles from somewhere in my stomach. It's not directed toward anyone—I think it's just excess emotion, but that almost makes it worse. Is this how life is going to be from now on? Hot and itchy and always in this painful space between yelling and tears? Calum said he didn't want what happened at home to affect my relationship with Mom and Dad. They didn't hurt him on purpose. I know they didn't, but hurt is hurt no matter why it occurs.

Mom looks as defeated as I feel. She swipes a hand over her eyes. After a pause, she jerks her head toward the flat. "We can talk more about this later. I don't . . . want to linger here longer than necessary. Go pack your things—we're staying in a hotel on the other side of the city until our flight home on Monday."

"No!" The exclamation slips out before I can help it. When they said we were leaving, I didn't realize they meant *right now*.

"Maisie," Mom says warningly.

I open my mouth to fight, to yell that they can't drag me away before I've even said a proper goodbye. But then another thought hits me. A more important thought.

"You can't stay in London until Monday."

Mom swipes at her eyes again. "Maisie—"

"Calum doesn't want you here."

"London is huge," Dad says. "We won't—"

"He doesn't want you here." I breathe in, trying to control myself. If we stay in a hotel in London, I won't have to say goodbye just yet. I can meet up with Calum in the evenings, and we can be in the same place for the video project launch on Sunday.

But I saw Calum's face when he found Mom and Dad on his doorstep.

I force my tone into something more reasonable. "I—will come with you," I say haltingly. "I'll come without arguing. I'll pack my things right now. But only if we stay at Aunt Lisa's until the flight."

Mom hesitates. She glances at Dad, and they seem to have a silent conversation before turning back to me.

"I'll ring Lisa," she says slowly. "And Dad—"

"I'll check the train schedules and try to cancel the hotel reservation," he offers.

Mom nods and takes a step toward the curb. "We'll leave you to pack. If everything goes to plan . . . we should be ready to go to Scotland in a few hours."

I breathe out slowly. Maybe they realized I'm right about giving Calum space, or maybe they're just seizing the opportunity to get me home without more screaming. Either way, it's a win. "Text me when it's time to go," I say. "Don't ring the bell. I'll meet you outside."

They both give me tentative smiles. I'm not ready to return them, so I just nod once and walk inside.

Hello, Goodbye

When I reenter the flat, Benji is cleaning up the mess in the living room. "Where's Calum?" I ask.

"Gone."

"What? Where?"

Benji shakes his head. "He hopped the fence out back. Said he needed air."

"When's he coming home?"

Benji shrugs and then shrugs again. He looks anxious and upset; I walk over and nudge his arm. "My parents are leaving. We're going to Scotland. Tonight."

He sets down the trash bag with a plop. "All of you?"

I nod. "We're flying back to New York on Monday. I convinced Mom and Dad that we should stay with my aunt until then."

Benji goes to pick up the trash; I push his hand away. "I'm going to hug you goodbye. I don't want to do it while you're holding garbage."

"Now? You're leaving now?"

"Soon. I've still got to pack my stuff."

He chews on his lip. Then he grabs his phone off the couch. "Calum doesn't know you're leaving. He'll want to say goodbye."

The call goes straight to voice mail. Benji shakes his head. "He'll want to say goodbye," he repeats.

I nod. "I'll wait as long as I can."

•••

It's not long enough. Rose went out to get pizza and Benji's still cleaning, so I pack my room by myself. It's weird being alone after a summer of so many new people. The past few weeks were exhausting, but I liked the constant noise. It will be hard to get re-used to the quiet.

Two hours later, Mom texts that she and Dad are on their way. I drag my suitcase into the living room and join Benji and Rose at the kitchen table. It's covered in pizza, but no one moves to eat it. It was supposed to celebrate all the work we put into the Glenna's project—a project that would have died on my camera roll without Calum. We can't eat it without him.

July 22, 7:42 p.m.

Mom: We're outside.

I hold up my phone for Benji and Rose to see.

They glance at each other; Benji is biting on his lip again, and Rose's eyebrows are low on her forehead. I try for a smile, but even without seeing it, I know it looks forced.

I hug Rose first. "Thanks for letting me sleep on your floor. It was actually pretty comfortable."

She squeezes me tightly. "You're welcome to visit anytime. I hope things work out with your shop."

"Thanks."

I hug Benji next. "When you open the iPad, you'll see I've sketched your statues."

He lets out a surprised laugh and hugs me tighter before letting go. "I'm honored. Did you include a cape?"

"There are three options. You can pick your favorite." I pull away and grab my suitcase, trying to ignore the sinking feeling in my stomach. "Goodbye" is really just a moment at the end of something. It doesn't matter as much as all the moments that come before it, so there's no point in getting worked up when it doesn't go to plan.

But it's one thing for an ending to be disappointing: it's another to not get one at all. I didn't get to say goodbye when Calum left six years ago. I at least thought we'd get the chance now.

My insides squeeze. My eyes itch. I duck my head as I walk through the front door for the last time.

As I go, I text him.

> Me: Went to Edinburgh with Mom and Dad and I don't think we're coming back.
> Me: Don't make me wait another six years to see you again.

Then I'm gone.

Silence Is the Worst
(Except When It Isn't)

No one talks on the train to Edinburgh. I stare out the window at the dark sky and the few sheep visible in the moonlight, and spend the whole ride trying not to cry. It's ridiculous. I didn't even want to come to the UK, let alone spend time with Calum. But this is just so abrupt, in the same way it was when Mom and Dad sat me on our living room couch all those years ago and told me my brother was gone. It didn't process at first. I thought they were joking, because how could he just leave? How could someone be a part of your life and then not be anymore? What were you meant to do with the echo they left behind?

We meet Aunt Lisa at the train station, and I grab her in a hug. I didn't really get to know her this summer, at least not in the way I was supposed to. But there's something about her. I could live in her arms.

"Good to see you, hon," she says as she holds me. When I finally let go, she gives Dad a nod and Mom a weird bro hug. It's so awkward that I almost laugh, but I don't, and we all lapse into silence until Aunt Lisa jerks her head toward the road. "Shall we?"

•••

It's past midnight when we're all settled into Aunt Lisa's flat, so I go to bed without saying good night. Mom and Dad are sleeping on the fold-out couch, and I'm back in the spare room.

Since we're only here a few days, I don't bother unpacking. I just kick off my shoes, pull out my pajamas, and slump into bed. It's hot and hard to breathe when I slip beneath the covers, but that's no different from how it feels without the blankets. A light pierces the darkness. I nearly jump out of my skin until I realize I'm still holding my phone. When I glance at the caller ID . . . oh.

I put the phone to my ear. "Hi."

"Hi," Calum says. "I had my phone off."

"Yeah." I pause. "Bad timing."

"You could say that."

I close my eyes, but the light from the phone still pierces through my lids. "Are you okay?"

There's another pause. I can almost see him running a hand through his hair. "Benji told me you went to Lisa's so they'd leave London. I . . . Thank you."

I'm silent. There isn't anything to say.

Calum doesn't say anything, either, but neither of us hangs up. Maybe this is what it will be like from now on. We won't be in the same house or even the same country, but there will be an open line between us, a pulse that never fully goes away. It's comforting, in a sad kind of way.

"Is the launch still happening on Sunday?" I ask finally.

"Eight o'clock," he confirms.

"Cool."

"Cool."

A pause. Until: "I forgot what quiet sounded like."

I almost roll my eyes. "Quiet doesn't have a sound."

"It does. It sounds like 'Maisie isn't telling me I'm five thousand years old every two seconds.'"

"You aren't five thousand. You're a hundred and seventeen."

"How silly of me."

I curl onto my side. "Don't disappear on me again."

"How could I, when I need you to remind me of my old age?"

"I'm serious."

"I know." Silence. Then: "I won't disappear, Maisie. I promise."

I lie in the darkness for a while. I don't remember falling asleep.

When I wake in the morning, I'm still holding my phone.

Maybe I'll Run Away and Live in a Castle Since There Are Like Eight Hundred Abandoned Ones in Scotland

Breakfast with Mom and Dad is super awkward, so when Aunt Lisa suggests going to Dunnottar Castle just the two of us, I jump at the opportunity. The ruins are a few hours north of Edinburgh and sit on a massive cliff overlooking the sea. We walk along the water, and I poke at the foam that forms in the waves near the shore. A salty breeze hits my face; I manage a smile as I crane my neck at the castle remains.

"Wow," I keep saying. "Wow."

"It's something, isn't it?" Aunt Lisa is wearing a dress covered in ocean patterns. It billows around her in the wind. "I often come here when I'm sad or need a think."

I can see why. This place is so beautiful that for a moment, I almost forget the rest of the world exists.

"We can talk," Aunt Lisa continues. "Or we can walk."

I hesitate, then sit on a big rock at the edge of the water. When the wind blows, waves break across the back, but it feels good to get splashed. I pull my knees to my chest and squint at the skyline. I don't know which direction we're facing, but if I look hard enough, maybe I'll see Crescent Valley.

I glance back at Aunt Lisa. When I woke this morning, I thought I wanted a break from reality. But I still have so much on my mind, and although I didn't get to spend much time with her this summer, the talks we did have were really helpful. "I'm feeling weird about going home," I say finally. "Calum said he doesn't want me to be involved in his stuff with Mom and Dad, but he clearly hasn't forgiven them. How am I supposed to forgive them if he hasn't?"

Aunt Lisa sits next to me. The waves are loud, but she doesn't raise her voice. I have to scoot closer to hear. "I was furious when Calum first arrived in Scotland," she says after a moment. "Fiona had been suffocating him, and I couldn't understand why she refused to listen to him. I told her I'd never forgive her, but . . . then I thought about it some more." She sighs, tilting her head into the salty breeze. "The truth is, forgiveness is a heavy word. When your parents disregarded Calum's feelings, they lost my trust. But forgiveness?" She shakes her head. "That's not mine to give or take."

Another wave crashes. Even though the water is violent, I suddenly feel a sense of calm. Part of why I've been struggling to figure out how to feel about my parents is because of exactly what Aunt Lisa said. I was focused on deciding whether or not to forgive them, but she's right: it's not my job to accept their apology. Only Calum can do that.

I braid my hair to give my fidgety hands something to do. "You and Mom seem okay now," I say hesitantly. "I mean, you're letting her and Dad stay at your house, so does that mean you trust them again?" As soon as I let go of my braid, the wind rips it apart. "What I mean is . . . how do you know when to trust someone?"

"Change doesn't happen overnight." Seagulls squawk overhead. Aunt Lisa waves goodbye as they fly toward the horizon. "When Calum first left home, your parents spent months apologizing. They even flew over here one summer while you were at art camp and waited outside my flat for hours in the hopes he would speak with them." She shakes her head. "They meant well, but once again, they were refusing to see that what they wanted was at odds with what Calum needed.

"It was only three years ago, after your parents started going to therapy, that I felt a change. Your mum rung and asked me to tell Calum that he was always welcome to reach out, but that she and your dad would stop contacting him. They earned some of my trust back for that."

I nod slowly. In some ways, I really do think my parents have tried to grow from their mistakes. They admitted they messed up with Calum, and I think a big reason why I was so shocked to find out how they treated him is because I could never imagine them doing the same thing to me. But they lied about why he left home. Were they *ever* going to tell me the truth? I'm not sure, and that's what still upsets me.

I close my eyes. Aunt Lisa hugs me against her. "Our family's a bit of a mess, but there are bright spots. I'm glad to have finally met you. You're wonderful, hon."

I wrap both arms around her and don't plan on ever letting go. But then another wave breaks and I jump. Aunt Lisa laughs. "We'll be soaked soon. Why don't we head up to the castle?" She takes my hand and helps me hop off the rock. As we turn away from the sea, the waves try to pull us back. But we're too strong to get sucked into the tide.

•••

The next day, Aunt Lisa takes Mom, Dad, and me on a tour of Edinburgh. We end up at the massive castle overlooking the city, where Aunt Lisa tells us about the cannon that still fires off the cliff every day at 1:00 p.m. Surprisingly, the tradition wasn't started as a reminder of war. It was used by ship captains to reset their clocks. Maybe that's why I decide this is the right place to reach out to Mom.

She's standing against a fortress wall, staring out at the city. There's no way to ease into this conversation, so I don't try to.

"I understand a little more," I say, stepping beside her. "I mean, about what happened six years ago. I know you never meant to hurt Calum and that you've spent a long time learning from your mistakes. But you hurt him again this week by showing up at his flat, and you hurt me by lying about why he left home. I get that I was little when he moved in with Aunt Lisa, but were you ever going to tell me the truth?"

Mom flinches and turns her gaze back to the city. I wonder if one of the rooftops we can see from here used to be hers. She grew up in Edinburgh, but I don't know specifically where. "Yes," she says quietly. "I always planned to tell you. But it wasn't as though everything happened at once. There were months of building tension between Calum and me, and then he left, and then there were months of thinking he would return. There were years of reaching out to him, and even more years of letting him go. I couldn't have explained the situation to myself back then—let alone to my six-year-old. And then I blinked, and you were this almost teenager who I knew would be more than capable of understanding, but I . . . worried you would view me differently. Poorly." She shakes her head. "I like to think I would have been honest eventually, but I can't be sure if I'd have found the strength. I'm sorry."

I meet her gaze. Her words don't really fix anything, but she gave more of an explanation than I asked for. I'm not entirely sure what that means to me, but I know it does mean something.

"I'm sorry, too." I jump a little when I realize Dad is standing on my other side. How long has he been here?

He peels his gaze from the sky and looks at me. His eyes are narrowed slightly, like it's taking effort to meet mine. "Mom and I have not been perfect." He lets out a grunt that might be the start of a laugh. "We're not even on the same playing field as perfect. But I can promise we will always listen to you. That doesn't mean you will always get your way—I stand by our decision to send you abroad, and I'm sure there will be many things in the future that we disagree on. But whenever you say something, it will be heard. We will consider it carefully, and if you feel we are not understanding it from your perspective, we will talk it through until we do." He nods, as though agreeing with his own words. "We can't change the way we treated Calum. But I can promise we will not repeat our mistakes with you."

I break his gaze and turn back to the skyline. I'm still mad. At both of them. I don't think that's going to go away for a long time, but now that Mom and Dad seem more willing to talk openly with me . . .

The cannon fires. I forgot that's what we've been waiting for, and I jump about two feet in the air when the sound booms across the city.

Mom puts a hand on my shoulder to steady me. I don't pull away.

I Don't Get Kidnapped Again

July 25, 1:35 p.m.

> Me: I MISS GERMAN.
> Me: AND SHEPHERD.
> Me: DON'T TELL SHEPHERD I SAID GERMAN FIRST.

Alicia: I would never.
Alicia: But I did tell them both you're coming home soon!!
Alicia: They started jumping for joy.
Alicia: Actually no.
Alicia: That might have been less about you and more because I was holding a bag of treats.
Alicia: Sorry.

> Me: Haha I'd jump for joy over treats, too.
> Me: I'M EXCITED TO SEE THEM.

Sunday is a mess of packing and travel plans. We're leaving early Monday morning for Heathrow Airport in London, so Mom and Dad spend most of the day making sure all our bags and documents are in order. It's so chaotic that I completely forget to tell them about my video project until three minutes before it's supposed to go live.

"Uh, hello?" I sprint into the living room. Aunt Lisa and my parents are talking on the couch; I shove my laptop in their faces. "There's a thing—I mean, I made a video—I mean, *look*." I've pulled up all of Calum's social medias, but his website is front and center on my screen since that's probably where my video will get the most views.

"Calum has a web comic that gets like half a million views a month," I'm finally able to explain. "I made a video about art and Glenna's that he offered to post on his site, and it's about to go live. I know you're planning to close the shop, but this might change things."

Mom and Dad glance at each other. "Calum helped you with this?"

I nod. "He said we all put parts of ourselves into the shop and it's where he fell in love with art."

Mom and Dad share another look, but they don't say anything. Aunt Lisa puts an arm around my shoulders.

I refresh the page.

My video appears. The moment it does, I text Calum.

8:00 p.m.
Me: It's live.

He doesn't respond. I text again.

Me: Hello?!
Me: You're watching this, right?!

The video went live less than a minute ago. It's ridiculous to assume he's disappeared on me—especially because he promised he wouldn't. But why isn't he responding? He knows how important this is. For Glenna's and for me.

I glance at my phone again. It's been ten minutes and there aren't even typing bubbles. Aunt Lisa nudges my arm. "Aren't you watching?"

"Huh?"

She points at my laptop. I've been so focused on my phone that I didn't realize how much was happening online.

I didn't expect we'd get responses immediately, but I guess things move fast when 500,000 people visit your website every month. Within ten minutes, the views on the video are racking up. I click to Calum's Twitter to see a thousand people have liked the post and a ton have already commented they've signed up for our Patreon. Calum's Instagram is getting similar responses and engagement. My eyes widen.

"It's working."

"It's working," Mom mutters, leaning closer to the screen.

The results are good. Better than I ever expected. They won't save Glenna's indefinitely, of course. We'll need a steady source of income for that. But they're a Band-Aid we can rely on while Mom and Dad look for a new investor. We might even be able to use people's interest in the video to prove there are customers who believe in our products.

Speaking of . . . "There's something else," I say hesitantly, and pull up the comic Calum made for this week. The panels are mainly there to introduce the video and the Patreon, but they also explain some of my ideas for adding digital portraits to the shop. "I don't want to change the heart of Glenna's. We'll keep doing oil paintings, of course. But I've been trying digital art this summer and I really love it, and it's a more accessible art form and . . . stuff . . ." I trail off. I should have practiced this pitch.

I expect my parents to be angry that I posted my expansion ideas publicly without asking them first, but Dad pats my arm and smiles without looking up from the screen. "We'll have to look into whether it's feasible, but I like where your head is at."

I bounce a little on the couch.

The numbers rise some more. Mom looks like she might cry. Aunt Lisa laughs and gives me a huge hug. I grin, but even though the video is working . . .

My phone stays silent.

●●●

I'm in bed for the night when I finally get a text. I'm so annoyed that I almost don't look at it.

10:57 p.m.

Calum: Come downstairs.

Me: . . . I'm in Edinburgh.

Calum: I know.

I frown, sliding into slippers and a pink hoodie. It's 11:00 p.m., and the excitement for Glenna's took a lot out of everyone, so I have to tiptoe past my sleeping parents on the couch in order to reach the door. When I open it, light floods in from outside. Dad grunts and rolls over, but neither he nor Mom seems to wake up.

I creep down the steps and into the shop. Unique Sweets is kind of creepy at night. A cool breeze drifts in from the door, and—

Shouldn't it be locked?

I almost bolt back upstairs to tell Aunt Lisa. But then I see him.

"Calum?"

My brother leans against the front window of the shop, right next to the open door. When he hears me, he turns around and nods.

I frown, but walk outside. "What are you doing here?"

"I couldn't let you go back to Crescent Valley without saying a proper goodbye." He holds up his phone. "Sorry for not responding to your texts. I was driving."

"I . . ." I don't know what to say.

Calum jerks his head toward the street. "I can't stay long."

"Are you going back to London *tonight*?"

"I've work tomorrow."

I stare at him. "Did you really come all this way just to spend a few minutes with me?"

"Maybe. So stop gawking and walk with me."

I hesitate. "What if someone realizes I'm gone? They'll really think I've been kidnapped this time."

"Lisa knows I'm here." Calum nods toward the street again. I follow him outside, even though I'm in slippers and pajamas. He's in a suit. On a Sunday. At 11:00 p.m.

Sometimes I really can't with him.

●●●

This city is always beautiful, but there's something magical about it at night with all the cobbled stones and soft streetlights. We walk in the direction of the New Town and stop on a bridge that straddles both sections of the city.

"How's London without me?" I ask.

Calum rests his elbows on the railing, looking out at the lights below us. "Buildings are burning. Swans are fleeing. The London Eye collapsed into the Thames."

"You're so annoying."

"You mispronounced 'hilarious.'"

"Never."

Calum clasps his fingers together. "How did it go with Glenna's?"

I give him a look. "You already know. The numbers are great—thanks to your website, we even have five thousand Twitter followers for the shop now."

"I meant with Mom and Dad. Were they . . . do they think it's enough to stay in business?"

I watch him carefully. "It's too early to tell, but they seemed excited. In just the past few hours, we've had more new orders for portraits than we've had in the last three months combined."

He nods. "Hopefully you can keep the momentum going until a new investor signs on."

"Yeah." We lapse into silence, until—

"Oh." I pull out my phone and bring up a screenshot I took of the Glenna's website. "Mom and Dad didn't realize you still cared about the shop. I told them what you said, about how it's the reason you fell in love with art. They did this a few hours ago. It'll stay up as long as Glenna's is around." I tilt the screen toward him.

Calum's eyebrows pull together slightly as he looks down at the phone. At the top of every page on the website is a text box. It's only one sentence, and the letters are pretty big. Even so, he blinks, like he's not seeing properly, then takes the phone from my hand so he can read it better.

"Five percent of all sales at Glenna's Portraits will be donated to LGBTQIA+ homeless youth shelters in Upstate New York."

Calum is silent for a long time. I stare out at the city below us. When I glance back, my stomach jerks. His eyes are very red.

I have no idea what to do, so I don't do anything. I just look away again and let him take his time with the web page.

Finally, he says, "I appreciate it. You can tell them. That I appreciate it." He hands my phone back and swipes at his face. When he lowers his arm, we make eye contact, and he blushes. "Those weren't tears," he mutters. "The wind is strong."

"There isn't even a breeze."

He rubs at his eyes again. "I ate something spicy."

"That's a worse lie than the *Shrek* bet."

He lets out a sharp laugh. "Pretty sure nothing can top the *Shrek* bet."

"You're right. I take it back."

We stand on the bridge for another minute or so, watching the cars and the people and the lights. Finally, Calum nods in the direction of the Old Town. "I'll walk you back."

"Already?"

"Sorry." His smile is dry.

We amble back to Unique Sweets in silence. I try not to think about how this is it, how for all I know, I might never see him again. Okay, that's ridiculous. I know I'll see him at some point. But when? We don't even live on the same continent.

We stop by the door, but neither of us moves to enter. After a moment, Calum gestures at the painted front window. "Did you know I did that?"

"Really?"

He nods. "Not my best work, but it's Lisa's fault for letting a sixteen-year-old decorate her shop."

I examine it more closely. "The flowers are a bit wonky, but I like the colors and the lettering."

"Thank you, esteemed art critic."

"Anytime."

Calum takes a step toward the road. "Well—"

"Don't leave." My voice breaks, and I don't care. I run forward and hug him, and I don't care.

He wraps his arms around me. "You can visit anytime." His voice is slightly muffled by my hair. "I have a fancy job—I'll pay for your plane tickets."

I make a noise somewhere between a sob and a laugh.

"I'm serious," he says. "How's Christmas? You get two weeks off school, right?"

I pull away. "Really? I could come for Christmas?"

He gives a single nod. "Really."

I don't want to get emotional right now because let's be real, my emotions don't just need a break—they need a full-blown vacation. But the thing about siblings is that they don't have to like you. Not in the way your parents are supposed to. Calum didn't have to reach out to me. He doesn't have to care about me. But he did, and he does, and that matters. It's everything.

I hug him again. "Try not to get too old while I'm gone."

"You should be more concerned that I'll end up in a basement somewhere. They don't take kindly to leaked government secrets—and by 'they,' I of course mean the men in sunglasses who showed up at my door when I turned eighteen."

I smack his arm. "Are you a spy? Like, *actually*? Because at this point I'm ninety percent sure you are one. Blink once for no or twice for yes." I watch him closely.

He doesn't blink at all.

"You're so annoying!"

He tries to hold back a grin, but I see it in the dim light. "I'll miss you, too."

I huff out an exaggerated breath and turn on my heel without another word. I don't look back as I walk into the shop.

If I look back, I'll cry.

Epilogue

Unfinished

I'm sitting on the floor of the Glenna's workshop, reading through the new poems Alicia wrote for The Book this summer. The first thing I notice is that they're different from all the ones she's written previously. Although they range in subject from "German and Shepherd Run Circles in the Yard" to "My Heart Lies Forgotten in a Manure Bed," there is something about the overall tone that feels the same. They're cohesive in a way none of her earlier poems were.

"Well? Can you see them going in The Book?" Alicia asks. She's sitting on her hands a few feet from me, her teeth chewing at her bottom lip. I've never seen her look this worried while I'm reading her work, but I think it's the distance. We were so far away from each other when she wrote these—both physically and mentally. I put down the papers and look up at her. "I don't think so."

She flinches. "They aren't good enough?"

I shake my head quickly. "It's not that—they're great—it's just . . . " I pause. "They're so different from your other poems. And I didn't do any art to go along with them, so maybe they should go in a new book? Your own book?"

"No!" Alicia says. "Maisie, I love making art with you—"

"I don't mean we should stop making art together. It's just that these poems feel personal. To you. So maybe they should just be yours, like how the art I did this summer is mine."

Alicia hesitates. Then she nods slowly. "I see your point. But it means we have nothing new to add to The Book. Should we start on something today? We should at least commit to a real title. Or a theme. It so badly needs a theme."

My hands tighten around the raggedy old sketchbook we've been pouring our art into for the past three years. It's my most prized possession.

It's also a mess.

"I think we should start a new one." I first had the thought on the plane home to New York, and it's grown stronger every day since.

Alicia looks hesitant again, and I get it. It's scary to start something new. But I'm not the person I was before I left for Scotland, and even though Alicia spent the last few months in Crescent Valley, she also had an important summer. I think a change would be good for both of us.

"We'll put more thought into this one," I continue. "We'll come up with the theme before we start, and we won't put the finished versions of your poems or my paintings into the book until we've got an entire first draft. That way, we can arrange them in the order we want and make sure we're sticking to the theme."

Alicia makes a face. "I prefer writing straight in the book."

"I know. But—"

"Yeah, yeah." She rolls her eyes and grins. "A new book. It's growing on me." Then she frowns. "But what do we call it? It can't be The New Book."

I think for a second. "Let's wait on the name. At least until we know the theme."

"But it needs to be called *something*." Before I can give a suggestion, her face lights up. "Unfinished."

Oh.

We look at each other and grin.

Unfinished.

●●●

The next night, I'm alone in the Glenna's workshop. As much as I want to start brainstorming themes for Unfinished, I have a ton of portrait work to catch up on. Apparently Mr. Fluffer's portrait was such a success that Melinda Matthews recommended us to her friends at knitting club and they all ordered commissions.

The one I'm working on now is for Mrs. Thompson. She has six cats, and wants them painted like a family portrait, complete with her in the center. I've sketched an initial composition, but something is just . . . not working. I step away a few feet to get a new perspective. When that doesn't work, I lie on my back and look at the drawing upside down. This usually unsticks me, but when I shoot back to my feet, I'm just as lost as before.

I wipe graphite from the side of my palm, pick up my phone, and press FaceTime. When the call connects, I'm face-to-face with a black rectangle.

"Maisie," Calum growls from somewhere in the darkness. "It's three a.m."

"Oh! Sorry." I've been home for a month, but it's still a constant struggle to remember Calum and I aren't in the same time zone anymore. This is the third? fourth? time I've called him at an unreasonable hour.

"What do you want?" he asks.

"It's fine. Nothing important. We can talk tomorrow—"

I hear shuffling, and then footsteps. A door opens and closes, a light switch clicks, and suddenly I see Calum's scowling face. "I'm already up," he mutters, shoving glasses he only wears at home onto his face and flopping onto the living room couch. "What is it?"

"It's not important—"

"Maisie, I swear to—"

"Right, okay. Look." I flip the camera to show Calum the sketch. "Why isn't it working?"

He leans forward, squinting through the screen. "Why on earth are there so many cats?"

"Mrs. Thompson," I say by way of explanation.

"Ah." Calum tilts his head to the right, then to the left. "Maybe it's . . . too realistic?" he suggests. "It's not that the composition is bad, but I remember Mrs. Thompson's house—all of the art on her walls was surrealist. Maybe you should lean into that?"

Oh, he's totally right. I can't imagine Mrs. Thompson hanging a traditional-style portrait in her house next to her painting of a flower pot full of cats or the cat-bus print she has from the movie *Totoro*.

"What if I change the scale?" I ask suddenly. "I can make the cats human-sized and Mrs. Thompson cat-sized?"

Calum's lips quirk up. "I think she'd be into that."

"Cool. Thanks for—" I jump as the door to the workshop slams open.

"Maisie?" Dad crosses the threshold, a bucket of paint in each hand. "You shouldn't be working this late at night. Come on back to the house." He sets down the paint with a grunt and glances over my shoulder. "Calum?" he says in surprise. "What time is it in London?"

"Three a.m.," he mutters, running a hand through his static hair.

"My fault," I say. "I forgot the time difference again."

Dad smiles tentatively at the phone. Calum hesitates, gives a single nod back, then stifles a yawn with his elbow. "I'm going to bed. Bye, Maisie. Talk later."

"Bye!"

My phone goes dark. I shove it into my pocket as Dad jerks his head toward the barn doors. "Coming?"

"Right." I scribble a note at the bottom of my sketch— *human-sized cats, cat-sized human*—so I don't forget the new plan overnight. Then I set down my pencil and follow Dad out of the workshop.

Things have been quiet between us for the past few weeks. As we walk back to the house, I ask tentatively, "Are you nervous for tomorrow?" He and Mom have a meeting with an investor in New York City. If it goes well, Glenna's will have funding again.

Dad shakes his head. "I have a good feeling about this one. Besides, if it goes badly, we'll just try again."

I look out at the dark horizon. I'm not as convinced that we'll get this investment as he is, but I have no doubt he and Mom will keep trying if it falls through.

"Speaking of Glenna's, Mom and I have been thinking . . ." Dad pauses.

My stomach flips.

The last time someone started a sentence with that tone of voice, I ended up in another country. I guess Dad can see the panic in my eyes, because he gives a small smile and places a hand on my shoulder. "Don't worry. You'll like this."

"Okay?"

"Mom and I have been thinking more about your idea of selling digital art products at Glenna's," he continues. "We'd like to start small, offering one type of portrait at a set cost. But if it goes well, we can discuss expanding to include more of your ideas. Neither Mom nor I knows how to do this type of art, so you'll have to take on most of the responsibility. It will be a lot of work on top of school, but we'll treat it like a job and pay you. Does this sound like something you'd be—?"

He's not able to finish his sentence before I leap into the air and scream, "YES!"

He laughs. I grin so wide that my cheeks hurt, and I do an awful attempt at a ballerina spin that ends with my butt in the grass. Dad laughs harder, and soon I'm cackling, too. We're still laughing as we walk into the house, kick off our shoes, and join Mom in the living room for a late-night movie.

Acknowledgments

This is a quiet book, but it had some very loud cheerleaders. I'm so grateful to everyone who believed in it, who told me to keep going, and who reminded me I was being ridiculous every time I wanted to throw my laptop out the window in writerly despair.

Thank you to my agent, Megan Manzano, who took a chance on this story right when I was planning to take a break from writing. Publishing is a difficult business. It's easy to convince yourself that no one will ever be passionate enough about your stories to give them a chance. But then you came along, and I'm still pinching myself.

Thank you to my editor, Mari Kesselring, for helping me find the heart of this story and for understanding the characters so deeply. And to Victoria Albacete: your enthusiastic comments and spot-on editorial notes added so much to this book.

Thank you to Emily Temple for marketing and publicity, Jake Slavik for book design, and Ana Bidault for illustrating my absolute dream cover. To everyone at Jolly Fish who worked on and advocated for my book: you are a fantastic team and this experience has been so wonderful!

This novel started as my senior thesis at Hamilton College. Thank you to Professor Anne Valente for giving me the space to write the story I wanted, and for being supportive of the messy first draft. Shoutout to my fellow Creative Writing seniors in that class: your thoughtful comments and critiques made this book so much better.

To my beta readers: Trisha Kelly, Adrianna Cuevas, and Britney Shae Brouwer. Esme Symes-Smith: you deserve your own sentence because I made you read the book at least three times. Natalie Crown: thank you for reading the whole thing in a day and yelling about it in my DMs.

We're always told not to befriend strangers on the internet, but even though I haven't met most of my #llamasquad in person (or heard your voices or ever confirmed you're not in fact a literal group of llamas): I was so alone in this journey before I met you. Thank you to Catherine Bakewell, Kiana Harris, Sarah Jane Pounds, Makayla Sophia, Megan Lynch, Marina Hill, Cyla Panin, Katie Knightley, Susan Wallach, Nicole Aronis, Rachel Greenlaw, Katherine Holom, Lillie Vale, Ashley McAnelly, Melissa Bowers, Jacy Sellers, Adriëlle Blaas, Trisha Kelly, Jania Johnson, Katy Lapierre, Erin Madison, Lenore Stutz, Mary E. Roach, Lisa Matlin, Sarah Fowerbaugh, Rochele Smit, Gabriela Romero Lacruz, Alaysia J., Aurora Martinez, CT Danford, Dory Goode, Christine Jorgensen, and Rachael Williams. I would not have wanted to do this without you.

Paige Pendergrast: you've read this book (and all of my books) so many times. Thank you for always putting up with my writerly angst (and my general angst. I am an angsty human). Kylie Winger and Halsey Stultz: you made Edinburgh so wonderful. I probably wouldn't have written this book if I didn't miss it so much.

Mom and Dad: You've believed in me since day one (even though I still haven't let you read anything I've written). Thank you for giving me the space to be creative, and for never once telling me not to pursue my dreams. Mitchell: you might not be a writer, but you know books and are always great at helping me fix mine.

Finally, to the cats: Lily, Lucy, and Crookshanks. Yes, it was sometimes difficult to write when you were sitting on my chest or laptop keyboard, but I don't care because you are so cute and fluffy.

About the Author

Sabrina Kleckner is the author of *The Art of Running Away*, a middle grade contemporary novel about family and identity. She began writing at the age of twelve, and is grateful not to be debuting with the angsty assassin book she toiled over in her teens. When she is not writing, she can be found teaching ESL or gushing about her three cats to anyone who will listen.